Escape in 1948

And Other Stories

B.W. Wilson

To Woody, Our Dog

You will always be in our hearts.

Thank you to The Heather Gardens Writer's Group

who helped me focus.

Table of Contents

THE SILENT ESCAPE

Late in 1948, after the Russians closed the borders to Czechoslovakia, enclosing the country behind the Iron Curtain, this story begins and deals with a small band of patriots who planned to escape. Many at this time were trying to flee the country and its abuses, but few were successful. This group of fifteen was determined to run the gauntlet for freedom, no matter the risks. If they were caught, it might result in death, but ordinarily, it would mean internment at hard labor in some work camp for the rest of their lives. These brave souls were together in spirit and resolute in their decision despite the danger. They understood what they were attempting could cost them dearly, even their lives.

The escape plan included their traveling for five or six nights on foot across country roads, highways and cultivated fields in complete silence without being noticed until they reached the border with Germany. Then they would have to make a dash for the security fence, cut a hole in the barbwire and run for cover. Including their tremendous fear of something terrible happening, this was a formidable task.

In the group were a two-year-old girl named Lottie and her three-year-old brother named Helmut, their mother and father, a single middle-aged woman named Elizabeth, her nephew Samson, his girlfriend Frieda, Hans, a retired school teacher, a farmer named Gerhosh, his wife Martina and sister Veronica, two male university students Patrick and Jakub plus a street-car driver from Prague named Martin. The elected leader of the group was Victor Mann, a forty-eight-year-old forester from the suburbs of Prague. He was a single man who had a kennel of pedigree hunting dogs. His plan was to bring along a dog, one of his youngest, not fully trained, named Fljot. Fljot (pronounced Floott) is Czech for swift of foot, or swift runner, as explained by Victor.

The escapees made plans to travel at night and to sedate the children, sleep in garbage cans if they had to, and sneak through back alleys, junkyards or wherever they could find a hiding place during the day. It would require cautiously executed plans to find their way to the border with Germany. What gossip they heard included the number of other patriots running this same risk every day who were getting caught. This was the kind of news that struck fear in their hearts. The question they were all thinking was: could they make a successful escape taking the children along?

The team started out the first night walking to the outskirts of Prague, where they assembled at the house of a good friend of Victor Mann, the leader. She fed them a good meal and gave them additional items she had stockpiled, such as cheese, bread, dried apples and a goodly amount of dried beef for their journey. They hoped to find good drinking water along the way, so the householder gave them some very scarce coffee to take with them.

The next evening, they started out traveling on the road and it was a very frightening time for everyone. This was an entirely new experience. Their job included getting accustomed to all kinds of sounds, lights and shadows. The route went along an old farm road, taking them in a westerly direction to Germany, they hoped. Some talk they heard was it would be easier to cross the border into Germany than anywhere else. Much excitement and anxiety occurred each time a car or truck approached when they jumped into the ditch, holding their breath and waiting until the vehicle passed. Keenly alert, marching along in single file, wondering who was going to catch them, gave them chills of anxiety. The parents with the children were in the middle of the column, where they were better protected. No one knew how far they had traveled, but they spotted an old barn that wasn't too far from the road and it was going to be their next stop just before daylight. They settled down on the straw floor, opened their blankets, ate a snack and fed the children who were hungry and needing attention. Fljot stood guard at the door of the barn as they all settled down to sleep.

The children were difficult to put to sleep again after being drugged for the night's walk, yet eventually they fell asleep. However, they were awake and ready to play by 7 a.m. in the morning. While being slightly sedated, they had slept the previous night on their parent's backs, where they were strapped. Now what to do with two rambunctious children? The two were sweet youngsters and they were totally in the dark about what was happening. Perhaps thinking this was some kind of game they were playing, their mother actually whispered something to them like that, but now they were awake and ready to play. The farmhouse was approximately five hundred meters up the road from the barn, so they had to be quiet. The escapees couldn't afford anyone hearing them and being discovered. Not one person in the area could be trusted. Russian sympathizers were everywhere and any peasant in the countryside could be a risk to the group if discovered.

The group survived the day in the old barn without detection. The escape party snacked on a few goodies they had brought with them and at 7 p.m., they were ready for another night's journey. Victor Mann estimated they were eighty or ninety kilometers from the border and that they should get on their way soon. They studied their map and decided to follow another farm road that went in a westerly direction. One of the university students recognized the road since he had worked as a delivery driver for a company that serviced this area. He spoke up and told Victor they needed to be extra cautious about making sounds. The children were once more sedated with phenol-barb and strapped tightly to their parent's backs. Victor went out by himself to check if the coast was clear. He took Fljot with him and in a few minutes, he returned with a grin on his face, indicating he was ready to get started. The team was excited to be on their way again. Every minute spent waiting was beginning to play on their nerves and cause them more anxiety and fear.

This night, they divided into two groups with the idea that if one group was caught, the other group would have a chance to get away. The children were in the latter group for their protection. They had a good time and again, when they saw headlights on the road, they would jump into the ditch. This particular road was more traveled and their progress slowed. As they approached a small village, the two groups rejoined and discussed their strategy to get through this town. From a distance, they could see the village in the dim moonlight. The sky appeared sinister and chilling. They decided they would walk through the village in the shadows rather than going around. The village town was only two blocks long and there were no streetlights. The moon was partially hidden by the cloud cover, which reinforced their decision to go through rather than circling around. Following their plan would eliminate many of the potential hazards of stumbling around in the cultivated fields and waking up the community. Having measured the risks, they decided this plan would help them stay on schedule.

Breaking up into teams, Victor was out in front with his dog. Fljot was barely trained. He was a young seven-month-old registered English Setter with white fur and just a few black spots showing through his magnificent coat. Fljot was the offspring of champion show dogs Victor raised at his home just outside the city of Prague. Many of these breeds are raised for hunting birds; however, they can be trained for many things due to their intelligence. Victor had taught Fljot only a few commands, such as to search and to return. Victor would point and give the command, "Seek," and Fljot would head out in the pointed direction. Most of these types of dogs will naturally spot game and freeze in place, pointing their nose directly at their prey. They are excellent at this with very keen sight and smell. Of course, in the dark, it was hard to see Fljot and what he was doing. A few minutes later, he would give a whistle, and Fljot would return. That night, Fljot earned the respect of the group as they watched him search the street ahead. It appeared when he returned wagging his tail, there was no one he detected.

The ghostly-looking troop, all clothed in black, made it through town, slowly walking in the shadows even though there were two occasions when dogs were heard barking at their presence. At midnight, no one is interested in getting out of bed to check a barking dog. Thank God, no one did. As the last three in the group were almost through the final block and starting down the road, another farm dog startled them. It began barking and growling as it approached the Three. This unfriendly encounter would certainly wake up the town if this barking dog was not stopped and the dog kept approaching. The farmer and the two university students were the target of this German shepherd. He was not intimidated by the men and kept viciously growling as he approached. One of the students, Klaus, suddenly opened his backpack and took out a hunk of dried beef and threw it at the dog. As the dog grabbed the meat, the three ran up the road as fast as their legs could carry them. As they approached the ditch, they dove in head-first into the cold, wet, stinky mud. They could hear voices now in the town, but they didn't look back as they quickly marched down the road dripping wet. They were well out of town and in the background, they could hear a vehicle approaching, which sent chills up their spine. They looked at each other and mumbled, "Run for it!" and they ran for their lives into the woods. They waited only a few minutes, which seemed like an eternity. In the dim light, they could see a jeep with two men, one driving and the other standing with a spotlight in his hands. He was shining the light along the road and as they drove by, the light did not spot them. The jeep continued along for another quarter kilometer and returned very slowly, shining the light as they came to a stop in front of where most of the group was hiding. Everyone kept their heads down, burying them in the ice-cold muddy earth, not daring to take a peek. Their hearts were beating so hard that they thought the sound would give them away. Their dark-colored clothing, however, blended them into the darkness of the night. With no visible movement, the jeep pulled away while the men said something like "dumb dogs are always barking about nothing."

The team was thoroughly exhausted at this point and could have remained there all night, but this was not a good idea. Victor knew better and got them back on their feet for a few more hours. These next hours were the most miserable and frightening that night. Victor knew this was his only recourse for them to overcome their fright and to calm their spirit. It was approaching 2 a.m. and they needed to go another eight kilometers before they stopped at 5 a.m. They made good time and were on the outskirts of a large town by first light. Thankfully they had made it to the end of this leg of the journey, exhausted but thankful.

Victor knew their exhaustion and was on the lookout for a place to hide and sleep. He saw what looked like a junkyard where numerous old pieces of machinery and tractors were parked. It had a fence around it and it didn't look like a place frequently visited except during harvest time. There was a small tool shed that was locked, which looked like it could hold five or six people and some soft spots under the tractors that would be good sleeping sites as well. He gave the couple with the kids and the retired school teacher the tool shed to sleep. The others picked their spots and immediately curled up and went to sleep.

Around noon, Victor got up and looked around. He found a large drum of rainwater and filled everyone's canteen. He was the only one up and moving around in case he was being watched. He started a fire to cook some coffee. It was risky, but he appeared to be a loner camping out. Several vehicles and a wagon went by, which paid him no attention. He looked like just another wayfarer now that he was unshaven and dirty. About 5 p.m. as a hay wagon approached, Victor got up with his coffee cup in hand and waved at the driver. The wagon stopped and Victor went out to the road to meet the man. The driver was an older man and those hiding could hear them talking, but it was not clear what they were saying. The farmer had pulled off the road, got down from his wagon seat and sat down by the fire. Victor surprisingly spoke fluent German as well as Czech and they were talking briskly in both languages. It was getting darker and the fire was burning out when Victor began moving about the camp getting everyone ready for a wagon ride. It was past 7 p.m. and quite dark when they were loading aboard this antiquated vehicle. Victor did not have any discussion with the others about doing this ride but none voiced any objection. Even though the wagon was not as full of hay as it is at harvest time, sometimes piled ten feet high, there was enough remaining to cover the gang adequately. They were packed together like a cord of wood, but made as comfortable as possible and covered with the remaining hay left in the wagon. The wagon owner reminded them to cover their heads and faces with scarves or handkerchiefs to keep out the very irritating hay dust.

Victor Mann and his new friend, through circumstance, got up on the driver's buckboard seat and began to pull out of the junkyard. Upon getting to the main road, several official-looking black sedans drove by at that same moment and looked suspiciously at the wagon and its driver, but did not stop. It was a kilometer to the town of Beroun and most everyone would have been at dinner at this time of day. The wagon continued along on the rough cobblestone street, making unbelievable noise and to those in the wagon, the noise was deafening. Steel-reinforced wagon wheels rolling over granite cobblestone make for a rough and very uncomfortable ride. The owner of the wagon was a farmer from this vicinity and many people knew him. Consequently, he drew little attention or suspicion when he traveled around town. As they proceeded through town, the minutes passed very slowly for those hiding in the wagon. They felt buried beneath the hay and every minute was almost like eternity waiting for the next time they would stop. Below the hay pile in the dark, not being able to see, every noise is magnified a hundred times and is alarmingly suspicious. Just people on the street who are only a few meters from the wagon sound like they are about to climb aboard, which provokes fear in everyone. Fortunately, the children were sound asleep and oblivious to all that was happening.

The Wagoner did a good job navigating through town. He waved at a few people who tipped their hats to him as they made their way to the outskirts of town in about an hour. Victor had the driver pull over to the side of the road, where they lit up their hand-rolled cigarettes and continued like they were talking.

Actually, Victor was telling those under the hay to stay hidden a while longer since they had further to go to be out of danger.

They started rolling again down the road. It was easier than walking but not a lot of fun under the hay, which was penetrating every seam of their clothing and piercing each square inch of their skin. It was torture of a kind. Some, even in their misery, vowed never to ride in a wagon for the rest of their lives if they lived through this event.

The wagon stopped. Carefully, they dismounted, keeping a low profile once Victor gave the command and they got down on their stomachs. There were farmhouses in the area and they needed to be invisible. Victor suggested they eat whatever they had available, drug the children again and get back in the wagon. Heinrich, the wagon owner, it was learned, had been a veteran of the national Chezk army and was aware of who could be a problem for them if they were observed. He recommended he take them to a town further down the road, about ten kilometers, where they could find a better hiding place. They agreed, loaded back into the wagon with great apprehension, holding their breath as hay was placed over them again.

It was a strong horse pulling and Heinrich said he was the best he had ever owned. He had found him roaming around the countryside after the war. He had the markings of the artillery on his flank and Heinrich assumed he had been a pack-horse for the German army carrying munitions. He was very lean when he found him. And after Heinrich fattened him up, he regained great strength and could pull heavy loads. "Old friend" was what he called him and he became a close confidant for Heinrich, who talked to him constantly, asking his opinion on several occasions, as Victor remembered.

What happened to Fljot and where was he? The dog was very quiet through all this and part of the time, he walked alongside the wagon and the balance of the time, he sat on the seat with Heinrich and Victor. He was marvelously self-controlled and seemed to understand all that was happening. Fljot did not give any indication there was anyone under the hay. He loved the kids and would sleep with them each day, but he was being obedient to keep down and stay mostly out of sight. He acted like just another member of the team and was doing well on just a few dog biscuits each day. Victor recognized he had lost weight, but it was not a serious problem if he continued to drink lots of water, which he did in the ditch along the road as well as in the streams in the area.

Their current location was in a farming community probably forty to fifty kilometers from the border with Germany. The sunrise was slow and the cold made it difficult to move their mouths. Their lips felt frozen but they were trying to say their farewells to their new friend Heinrich. He gave them his lunch of bread and cheese and told them to be careful. The rumor he passed on was that the border police shoot to kill and ask questions later. He was a good man and he told the group if he did not have a wife at home, he would be coming with them. He was tired and frustrated with the communists and wanted to get away. He said, "Auf Viedersiegn," and he departed. They watched him go and as he approached the main road into town, two official-looking black sedans again approached and stopped. We could see him take off his hat and bow politely to the police. They got out and looked in his wagon, looked up the hill to where they were hiding and finally drove off. When the police were out of sight, he waved again to the fragile group and proceeded up the road.

The travelers were very cold and weary from their night's activity. They were hungry, so hungry their stomachs were growling. And it was time for a long nap, and in this particular location, they were able to observe their surroundings easily. The parents awakened and fed the children some of Heinrich's lunch. Everyone was in good spirits and excited about the eventual crossing at the border. These pilgrims were extremely tired from their exploitation under the hay. They needed their rest badly if they would have enough energy for the next day's journey to freedom. The parents assured everyone they would keep the children quiet until it was time to start again.

Because of the dense population in this area, they decided they would travel off-road as much as possible and again head in a Westerly direction toward the German border. The children were sedated once again and throughout the group there was a mixed feeling of joyous anticipation and real fear. They would be closer to the border sometime tomorrow evening and now, with some tepidness, they departed their safe hiding place for the open road, each one saying their prayers that God would get them there safely.

As soon as they got down the road a kilometer, they planned to walk across the field closest to the veldt or forest for concealment. A farm dog was alerted to their sounds and began to bark. Fljot was sent to distract the dog so they could get across the field before anyone could come to check out what was happening. In the distance, they could hear the dogs barking, but they were not coming in their direction, so they hurried on. Again the group traveled in two separate parties a hundred meters apart in the event the whole group would not be discovered at one time. They were doing well time-wise, but when Fljot reappeared, he was bloody about the neck from his run-in with the farm dog. Victor checked his wounds carefully and with his handkerchief, he washed the injury to his neck with water from his canteen and applied some ointment he had in his pack. Then the team of patriots were on their way again. The night sky was clear and the stars were looking larger than ever. Fljot was staying close to the group in front since his encounter earlier. His beautiful white coat was shown bright in the moonlight and then there was a gunshot that rang out very close to where the group was standing. The bullet was no doubt intended for Fljot because it hit the ground close enough to him that he jumped. He jumped again and scrambled for cover when another shot rang out. Victor looked around to see if he could determine where these shots were coming from. On the porch of a house about two hundred meters away, he could barely see someone. The group was frozen to the ground, where they had dropped down at the sound of the first shot. They could barely hear the voices of a man and woman talking. They found out from Victor that the man may have been the owner of the barking dog that was in the fight with Fljot. They overheard the man tell his wife he may have shot the dog and would check it out in the morning. They went back in the house and slowly, the team got on its feet and started on their way again.

The group traveled all night without another incident and was approaching another small village they could see in the distance. With light of the moon, they could see the church at this end of the village. The few houses lining the street with their chimneys smoking were a pleasant sight that made them remember their own houses back home. Oh how they wanted to stop. They were weary and totally exhausted from this forced march. Victor, realizing their condition quickly wanted to find a site for them to rest. He went alone with his dog Fljot and a half hour later, he returned with good news. He said, "We have to move closer to town and stay in a junkyard. He thought they could hide successfully there if they were careful. They agreed and they moved to this fenced location. There was a chain and lock on the gate, but Victor pulled on the gate and they squeezed in without waking the children.

All were through the gate in a flash. Now they must find suitable hiding spots for each member of the group. There was a lot of refuse, mostly junk, wooden boxes, crates and barrels scattered around and they quietly moved some of it to make places to lie down. They were so tired and in just a few minutes, they collapsed in place. Their food supplies were almost exhausted and only a few really had anything to eat. However, they shared the little they had, a half-pound hunk of dried-out cheese and a loaf of stale black bread was all there was, so they each had a bite. After eating a few morsels, they rolled over and went to sleep. Not even the stress of anticipating the events to come could hold back their eyelids. Their nerves were in shreds but the overpowering need for sleep drove them into the darkness of slumber. Oh! How good it felt to relax those muscles. The cool of the night air swirled around their faces, watering their eyes as they pulled their coats tight around their necks. The time was 5 a.m. on Saturday morning.

The night was peaceful as he looked up at the stars. Victor noticed several constellations he knew from childhood when his father pointed them out to him. His father told him many stories about these mythological constellations. Orion's belt's three stars and the stars making up Pegasus the horse were clearly visible. Those were peaceful times before the war when food was plentiful and people were happy. He wondered if they were going to make it to safety or die in some labor camp, never to be heard from again. He was uncertain and worried about their closeness to the border. He had heard stories from a few who had attempted this escape. A few got away! Others were not so fortunate and were captured, while some were shot. This is how it could end and what a tragedy it would be for them all. With this thought, fatigue overtook Victor and he crashed into a deep sleep.

In the morning, as he tried to awaken his aching body, the hazy winter sun blinding him, he tightened his parka as the Artic air pierced every bone in his body. It was the beginning of September and the nights were getting cold. He heard several vehicles pass by and then he heard his neighbors stirring and waking up. He whispered to Fljot, "Oh, how I wish I had a cup of hot coffee." This thought brought back to him all the wonderful coffee shops near his home in Prague. It made him depressed that he would never see Prague and his home again. But, here he was in charge of making major decisions that would reap consequences in the lives of his friends and now he needed to be their stalwart guide to freedom. He was nervous but got up smiling to be an encouragement to the others.

It had to be a little before noon; they were still tired and hungrier than ever. The children began to cry not far from him. "Haben zie ein bonbon?" (Do you have candy?) they cried to their mother. They were very tired because the drugs were wearing off, causing their little bodies to feel stressed. They were hungry and Victor decided to open his special reserves, a box of chocolates that he had saved for an emergency. The children did not know who he was since he had not talked to them, thinking he would keep them strangers and out of his realm of interest. He was worried that they might not make it for some reason, but here he was, holding both of them in his arms like a grandfather would and talking to them very sweetly. As he held them in his lap, he pulled the box from his pack and watched them out of the corner of his eye; he could see their eyes bulging out. There was excitement as he opened the box and both of their little hands were touching his hand as he reached into the box. It didn't take a second for the wrappers to be removed and the candy shoved into their mouths with delight. They looked up at him with a facial expression he would never forget. He kissed them both and gave the box to their mother.

Victor needed to discuss the plan for the coming night's adventure and their departure later that evening. The group was talking as he approached. He motioned for them to sit down. As he sat down, Victor looked at Martin, the streetcar driver, a man in his mid-forties. He asked him, "Will you do something for me? In the event we encounter the border patrol and I am captured. Would you be willing to lead the group to safety?" Martin assured Victor if alive, he would do his best to help the others get across the border. Victor asked the group not to be afraid, that this discussion was only if it became necessary. Victor asked him again to make sure Martin heard him correctly and Martin assured him he would take charge of the group if that time would ever come. Martin was a bit shocked by this request since he was not ready for any added responsibility for the group. He was honored though, that Victor thought so highly of him to entrust the whole group into his care in that eventuality.

Darkness was coming earlier each day. They started to pack up and get ready to move out. Fljot looked excitedly ready. The children were happy again, having a few sweets to satisfy their hunger. The sugar, however, would make them hyper and livelier, which could be a problem but what could the parents do? Their mother was responsible for getting them under control with the medication. It took about thirty minutes more for them to settle down. They were bundled up and strapped to their parent's backs. They were ready! Victor led them through the opening in the fence, smiling with confidence to each one as they passed through. Sensing his positive attitude, they were all encouraged. The plan was to walk around behind the town and straight for the forest; however, they had to go on for many kilometers. They walked in the dark, following the person in front for several hours without any disturbance and without stopping. They finally came to a small stream flowing through the center of the meadow that they were following. It was approximately ten meters wide and too deep to wade across. They had to find another way. Victor went south and Martin went north to find a crossing site. Victor and Martin returned almost at the same time with the news. Martin had found a wide spot in the stream that was shallow enough for the group to wade across. Victor had found a cattle crossing bridge half a kilometer away. This short delay made the group anxious. They were relieved with the news and ready to follow Victor to the bridge. This was a cattle grazing meadow and the distinct smell of cow dung was strong as they watched where they were stepping. The smell was not that offensive, considering the lesser danger following this path. They hunched down at the foot of the bridge, looking for any warning signs. Looking at Flote 'who was quiet and at attention, they quickly went across. They continued going southwest toward the border, following another country road and about midnight, they decided to take a short rest under some trees they noticed along the trail. The night sky was full of stars and they felt encouraged.

They passed the canteens around and drank heartily the fresh, cold water they had just retrieved from the stream. It was just what they needed to refresh themselves. Just then, they heard voices coming their way from across the field. Quickly, they got lower to the ground to conceal their location and fear of being caught gripped them. Squinting, they could see it was not the border patrol. There were about a dozen shadows coming straight for them. There was nothing they could do and in seconds, they would be discovered. When this new group were just a few meters in front, Victor decided to call softly so as not to startle them. They stopped dead in their tracks. Fljot rushed to meet them, wagging his tail, which was a sign to this party that he was friendly. Victor moved forward in their direction and spoke in Czech, "Don't be alarmed, we are fifteen from Prague on our way to Germany."

There was a big sigh of relief heard among both parties because they, too, were very fearful of the border patrol and the prospect of getting caught. They also had been on the move, traveling to the border for several days. Victor explained this to his group when he returned. Their leader had been a truck driver and was familiar with the roads going to Germany, where he had traveled delivering merchandise to retailers. He and Victor had agreed to travel following one another with the truck driver's group out in front since he knew the way.

It was another cold, dark night with an overcast sky and humidity you could cut with a knife. They were moving quickly along the shoulder of the road. Every now and then, they would have to jump into the ditch when headlights approached. It was comical in a weird sort of way, hearing the whole group at once crash into the ditch. It sounded like a herd of pigs jumping into a wallow. Victor was alert to this noise but it was what it was. This was no easy exercise and the danger was what you might encounter in the ditch in addition to getting soaked in mud. This was the domain of many skunks, badger-like animals and hedgehogs. The stench of these ditches was sickening and these animals were bad bedfellows. The group must have carried this strong order on their clothes since Fljot continued to avoid them.

When they stopped to rest, Victor went over to the other group and found out they were probably five kilometers from the border. Now they had to be extra careful not to make any noise and to spread out more so that they were not all bunched up. Maybe they would be more difficult to see if they were more disbursed. In the event they encountered the patrol, Victor instructed the group to run for it as best they could. If they all ran at once, then some would have a better chance of getting away. The Russian guards were regular guys but they got tired at night, especially when they had been on duty for twenty-four hours. They rotated shifts, but after many days of this guard duty, they needed a full night's rest to be totally alert. Victor's hope was that those on guard tonight would be half asleep when they came through. If they could get past them and into the forest, they had a much better chance of escape. So they were building up their confidence by encouraging one another with positive remarks in a whisper. "You can make it." "We have come all this far, what is going to stop us now?" "Remember what was said in the beginning: the risk is worth it and we can make it no matter what." "Look at how far we have come, don't give up hope and we will get to freedom tonight." They were getting more excited by the minute and more worried at the same time.

Moving on down the road in single file, everyone was very quiet and concerned about the outcome of this night's adventure. They were very frightened and for good reason. They could be captured, or worse, shot dead. They could be caught and imprisoned for life in one of the many work camps the Russians maintained in Manchuria. Fljot was visibly nervous going out to search the terrain and returning each time Victor would whistle. The whistle was a special instrument for animals that only they could hear. It is very high-pitched pitched and the frequency is not audible to humans. Victor sensed this uneasiness in Fljot and whispered to the group that they were approaching the border. The front group was moving along quickly and the rest were following behind. As they approached a bend in the road, the leading group was now all beyond the bend and totally exposed. There was a loud shouting command coming from a guard on the road fifty or so meters away, "Halt! Halt! Hande hoch oder ich schiesen," meaning hands up or I will shoot. At that same instant, they could barely see the dark outline of the soldier yelling at them with his automatic weapon in his hands.

The forward group bolted and charged into the field, running as fast as they could toward the fence. They ran for their lives and they could be heard thundering across the landscape, yelling to one another to jump a ditch or jump a fence. Eventually, the voices faded as they became more distant. There were a few shots fired in their direction but no pursuit could be detected. At this same time, everyone behind Victor followed his lead and slipped into the ditch, lying flat on their stomachs. They could hear the border guards now talking forty meters away. A few guards may have run off into the field to follow the first group. The bulk of the guards, however, remained on the road near their jeep. They took out their cigarettes and lit up. They were talking about the group they had just intercepted. After a half hour, they started their vehicle and proceeded down the road in the direction of the border check station.

Fear of being caught had a grip on everyone. They were paralyzed in the ditch. Only the nerve in Victor's neck was twitching and he hoped it wasn't noticeable. Everyone kept very still with his or her head buried in the cold mud as the jeep went by. A few minutes later, they came back past where the group was hiding and continued on, then turned around and proceeded back to the guard gate. After another five minutes, Victor lifted his head to look around. No guards were on the road, so he gently tapped each one on the shoulder as he went along the ditch while his other hand motioned for them not to speak.

Martin had a problem while lying in the ditch that needed his attention. He had a bowel movement and needed to discard his underwear and clean himself. Thankfully, he was able to get all this accomplished without alerting a guard. When he was finished getting his pants back on, he got everyone back on their feet and Victor motioned for them to move out. He followed the road, which was a surprise, knowing the border patrol was somewhere still on the road. Victor kept sending Fljot for short recon missions to scout out the road. His purpose was to check if there was anyone on the road or close by and each time Fljot returned, wagging his tail.

Finally, you could see the border crossing gate. About five or six guards were warming their hands over the fire burning in the oil drum. They were talking and smoking as if nothing had happened. Victor was highly alert, but remained calm as he instructed his group to get out of the ditch and run across the field while Fljot became a decoy in the other direction, distracting the guards. This was his best plan, considering the circumstances. They jumped out of the ditch all at once; adrenaline rushing through their veins they ran across the field faster than their legs had ever carried them. As they headed across the field, they could hear some loud voices and a few commands to shoot. Luckily, there were shots fired but not in their direction. Everyone made it to the barbed wire fence. It was poorly installed and with a few easy snips of the wire clips, they were through the fence and running for their lives another hundred meters into the woods. In the distance, they could hear the guards yelling at Fljot and another volley of gunshots.

Much to their surprise, they did not see or hear from any of the others in the first group. They hoped they got away. They themselves were exhilarated they had escaped with no one in pursuit. A few were praising God. With even more encouragement, Victor was able to prod them to march down a dirt road until they reached a small farmhouse. Victor knocked on the door while the others crouched down behind the barn. Some of these folks on the border were sympathetic to the Russians, so they were being careful. The residents were awake at this early hour and knew right away what was happening. Farmers close to the border had experienced this many times before. Many previous escapees had come knocking. The farmer invited this entire group into the large kitchen, warmly heated by the single stove in the house. Victor explained how they got there. The farmer's wife gently told the group to kindly remove their boots, and put them in the outside hall. As they settled around the room, she passed a warm pan of water so they could wash their hands and faces.

Next, she generously sliced Swartz brote (bread), a black bread that was particularly filling. It felt like a celebration of sorts, keeping them alert. After eating, everyone collapsed. All these loving kindnesses overwhelmed them and they began to thank her while crying from exhaustion.

What a relief to be safe and Victor was elated having gotten them to freedom. He was sad about Fljot though, who didn't show up after the shooting episode. Just in case he got away, Victor left his boots on the steps outside so the dog could pick up his scent. Fljot had done such a superb job with his decoy tactics that the guards did not have a chance to pursue the escapees. Everyone was thankful and gave God the credit again. If Fljot had given his all for the group, Victor would miss him terribly. When the team began to stir and awaken, they became aware of the dogs' absence. He was always in their midst and with the children. The consensus of their discussion was that God had overseen their flawless escape using the dog's courage. Fljothad made it possible and they believed the dog had given his life on their behalf.

As they warmed up in the kitchen, sitting on the floor, their eyes began to close once again. They were really worn out. While this was happening, the farmer's wife took the children upstairs to bathe them and get them some fresh clothes. She had a closet of clothes she had kept for her grandchildren, which would redress these children. Just then, there was a barking from outside the house. Victor jumped up excitedly from his very short nap and looked out the window. There was Flote looking at him. He looked a mess, bloody all over and mud caked an inch thick on his fur. Victor rushed out to greet him and took him into his arms. He had been shot in several locations but luckily, they were fleshy wounds and would heal once they were cleaned.

As they began to awaken from their nap, it was late morning and the US military police were on their way to pick them up. They were to be transported to a camp for refugees coming across the border. Camp Vechtschider would be their new home for the time being until they could find a country that would allow them to immigrate. Canada and the U.S of A were two of the better choices.

Fljot their hero, who was part of each of their lives, had become a faithful friend to them all. Victor would make the rounds through the camp and visit with each of the survivors every week, with Fljot in tow, greeting each person with his energetic self. Fljot remembered each one and would give them a sloppy kiss, especially the children who called Fljot their dog and wanted to sleep with him every night. This would be a difficult time for Victor since he would not be able to take the dog with him. Immigration would not allow any animal to immigrate with their owner.

Victor Mann was very attached to his dog and this information was heartbreaking. The camp director suggested he should begin his search in town for an American family who might be interested in the dog. There were many in the camp who desired the dog but they were in the same situation as Victor. He was not going to do anything until he found out when he might be leaving. After several months, he got the notice he was on the manifest for Canada and would be leaving in three months. Now, he must make this hard decision to find a new home for Fljot.

The town closest to camp, about ten kilometers away, was the town of Bad Orb. There were several military American families living there as part of the occupation. Victor decided to visit this town and see who might be interested in his dog. As he approached Bad Orb, he noticed two boys playing in the street. He went up to them and inquired if they knew of anyone who might be interested in his dog. The young American boys were quite excited to pet the dog and they told Victor they would like to have the dog but they must ask their father first for his approval. They told Victor he should come back that evening when their father would be there so he could see the dog. Barbara, their governess, came out of the house to see the man and his dog. She confirmed to Victor that Major Wilson would be home around 5:30 p.m. and he should come back then if he wanted to talk to him.

Victor arrived with Fljot at exactly 5:30 and knocked on the door. Barbara invited the man and his dog into the waiting area and went to get the Major. The boys, Billy and Rickie, were playing with the dog when their father entered the room and with Barbara's help in translating, a deal was struck. Victor would keep the dog in his possession and could bring

Fljot to the house on weekends to get him familiar with the Wilson family. At the same time, he could teach the dog some English. The Wilsons fell in love with Fljot making Victor's choice easier. He came weekly to continue to train Fljot for the next several months until he received his visa. It was an extremely emotional time for Victor to say his final goodbye to Fljot as well as his new friends, the Wilson family.

Mrs. Wilson, who was a volunteer with the Red Cross, was on the team looking after the needs of the people staying in the DP (displaced persons) Camp Vechtschieder. On occasion, she would take Fljot with her in the car when she visited the camp. She was helping with the delivery of supplies such as toiletries, blankets, socks and coats. Fljot continued to search the camp for Victor. For several additional months, some of the remaining folks of the Escape recognized Fljot and he recognized them. As the children had already immigrated, it seemed Fljot looked disappointed.

Fljot lived with the Wilsons and enjoyed their kindness for many years. The family loved their dog and for fifteen years, they transported him to many places around the world. Even when they went to Japan, they took Fljot with them. He was a real hit with the Japanese because of his beautiful white fur coat. Fljot was always the center of attraction and seemed to enjoy it. Everyone who came in contact with the dog loved him and conversely, he loved everyone as well. Interestingly, the story of Fljots escape from behind the Iron Curtain was seldom told in his lifetime. It was a sad day for the Wilsons when Fljot died. The family has never forgotten this wonderful animal. They still remember the talk about him and his wonderful temperament. Never had they owned a dog of this intelligence and beauty. They had many animals in the course of their lives, but after Flotie, as they were accustomed to calling him, never did they desire to own another dog. Any talk about this animal still evokes strong feelings for its owner and their sons, who still worship the memory of Fljot. He died at the age of 15 in human years and is still remembered by Billy and Rickie.

BRAZZAVILLE: REPUBLIC OF THE CONGO

"Out! Get Out! And get down into your positions. On the double! Get out! And get down to the perimeter." We had just landed at Brazzaville airport, and I was shouting to the men in my platoon to disembark the C-133 Globemaster aircraft as fast as they could. The engines were still running, and the cargo that was on a pallet, our machine guns, ammo, and rations, were going to be dragged out on the pallet all at once after we discharged the airplane. The extraction webbed cable was attached to our mule by the team, and all the men helped pull out the pallet. There were a few shots fired that we could hear from some distance away at the north end of the airstrip, but none close by. The jungle was all around this airstrip in 1964 when we landed there as part of an expeditionary force agreed to by our President Johnson to help the newly appointed revolutionary President De'Bat of the Republic of the Congo. Back then, we soldiers called it the Belgian Congo.

My platoon Sergeant, Duane, and I were attacking the tarpaulin to remove it for us to retrieve the contents when we came under fire. Just a few shots from a long way off, we went ahead and called for one squad at a time to come out on the tarmac and retrieve their M60 machine gun and several cases of ammo. It took two men to carry a case of ammo, and then the others carried a few cases of C rations. We were finished in twenty minutes, and by then, we had an audience of Congolese soldiers watching us. Watching only, not helping us drag all our supplies to the side of the tarmac, which was 100 yards away.

Once we were assembled off the tarmac, I decided to scout the perimeter while the men took cover and had a meal of C rations. Platoon Sergeant, Duane, and I checked out our Walkie-talkies, and they worked. Off I went, looking for the leader of the Congolese troops in uniform. Halfway around the perimeter, I found our illustrious leader who was Sergeant Kumba, who spoke fairly good English. He told me the main boss in charge was at lunch and could be back later after lunch and his siesta with his girlfriend. Wow! Didn't need all that info, but Sergeant Kumba was good enough to help me see the positions for the four M-60's. There were three places he told me that were most vulnerable and then the other M-60, we could put it anywhere we wanted. He said the rebels had been fairly quiet the past week, but knowing we were there would get them back to war. They were opportunist waiting for supplies to arrive before they would venture an attack. Their surveillance was excellent, and they knew everything that was happening.

Now, the fun started. Before I could get back to the platoon sergeant, my walkie-talkie was buzzing me. Duane wanted to know what to do with all the kids that were swarming around him and the pallet of rations. I told him to keep cool and that I would be there in 30 minutes. I was just beginning to see the whole picture and what we were going to do to protect ourselves. As I arrived back, I rounded up one squad and got them to cordon off an area 50 feet by 50 feet with yellow tape we had brought along. Then I told Duane to go and get Sergeant Kumba and bring him back to speak to these kids. He took off, and an hour later, Kumba arrived in a jeep with Duane.

I greeted Sergeant Kumba and gave him a cool drink of water in a cup that I had retrieved from the supplies. Kumba thanked me and then started waving his arms and raising his voice to the thirty children who had gathered. He later told me what he had told them. He explained, "General, I talk to young people and tell them danger to talk with green soldiers."

"Okay, why green soldiers?" I asked. He said, "You generals are green soldiers. You have green uniforms and black boots. We have brown uniforms and brown boots." (This took several minutes to understand)

Okay, I understand, but I am not General. I am Lieutenant. Call me that please."

"No, I cannot. You general and me Sergeant. You now boss." Boss of whatever he was telling me. I thanked him as I observed Sergeant Duane snickering as he was checking the pile of rations in front of us. I told Kumba that we would have some rations left over from the first few days and I would let him come with his jeep and take them to his troops and to the children. He joyfully nodded and said he would like that. Thank you, he kept saying as he got into his jeep. He said the kids would not get close to the rations again and, if they did, to call him.

Two rounds fired in the air was his call to come. One shot in the air was an enemy in the area. If I heard three shots in the air, it was to get ready for an assault by the enemy. One burst of five rounds meant we were under attack by the enemy and possibly some vehicles with mounted weapons. We were to commence firing when we heard this single burst of gunfire.

Now it was time to take my first squad out to the machine gun emplacement location and get them into position on the perimeter. The big problem was that these men did not have any way to communicate with me. I did not have any more Walkie-talkies for any of the squads. I explained to them this situation and maybe we could figure out some other way tomorrow. They got into position, and we discussed lines of fire, and then I was off to the next location for the second squad. I told them they could have my Walkie-talkie since they were the farthest away, and they thanked me profusely. The squad leader was really jittery, and I could see that. So, to help him get more comfortable with being out on the perimeter by himself with his squad, I gave him the telephone. I told him, "If you come under attack tonight and are sure you need help, meaning you are being overrun, call me, and I will bring the squad in reserve to help. We need time however to get here, so it will probably take 15-20 minutes going around in the dark." He said he understood, and off I went back to the platoon.

When I arrived back, I got Duane and told him what I had done, and he agreed with my decision to leave my Walkie-talkie telephone since we were so spread out. I told him to round up the third squad, and we both would take them to the critical location where the squad leader would need to be our most senior man. James was his name, and we indoctrinated him as to the S.O.P. Then Duane said he would stay out with the squad from the beginning and then he would get back to the platoon by midnight if all was quiet. If not, then he would stay all night. He gave me his Walkie-talkie, and after we designated the firing lines, we got with those few Congolese soldiers that were around in the area to show them our lines of fire. We walked them out a few yards into the undergrowth and explained with sign language how the lines of fire worked. They thanked us with nodding and smiles and more nodding. They then showed us where they were slightly dug in; they had dug out three to four inches as a firing position to lay down for the night.

That night became an interesting learning experience. Around midnight, I was at our first position, keeping an eye on things and was mystified by several sounds. In the dark, sounds travel really well and can be confusing. I thought several times we were facing rebels crawling on their stomachs. Strange noises, but not what I thought. In the morning, as the sun began to rise, I looked out, and there were chickens, small pigs, and other farm animals, like Guinea hens, digging in the ground. I was happy we hadn't lost our cool that night by firing our weapons. We would have disturbed the entire airport community. I was so proud of our team that I rewarded them with a soft drink I had ordered from Sergeant Kumba the previous day, and they were cool going down.

A couple of days went by with no excitement, and then in the afternoon of the fourth day, Sergeant Kumba came to me where I was trying to keep cool under a bush. He informed me there was intelligence he had just received that the rebels were getting restless and were going to attack the troops in green and steal their weapons, especially their machine guns. There was a weapon shortage, and the rebels needed more guns to outfit their new recruits. Machetes are not sophisticated enough weapons to keep the interest of the new warriors. These new recruits were still in their teens, I was told, and this was going to be their first fight. Woe is me, I thought. If these kid warriors were 4

not trained for this combat, then there would be many causalities on both sides. I was told they sometimes become fearless, and this can be devastating for both sides.

I thanked Sergeant Kumba and told him we had some extra C rations that we had for his troops. We loaded six cases, and I knew that we had money for some outside supplies and food products. I was going shopping with Kumba the following day and hoped to get us some bananas and whatever else I could find. I heard from one of the Congolese troops there was food available in the little village one mile away. Food like barbecue, he kept saying, but what kind was the mystery? I was going to wait until I tasted it to ask what it was. I was thinking it may be a possum or another animal like it we heard at night running around. I was not going to buy it if it was a monkey.

That afternoon, I warned the troops about the intelligence and that we should keep our cool again. I wanted them to check their weapons and keep enough ammo available for a fight. I told them the Congolese troops under Sergeant Kumba's command would be the first to engage their rebel counterparts, and then we could get involved as the fight heated up. Everyone nodded that they understood and tonight it would be important that two men stay alert at all times and be on a two-hour watch. This way, each soldier could get four hours of sleep before taking the watch again.

I asked Sergeant Kumba if he would do me a favor and drive me around to the checkpoints. This would save me an hour or more, and I could get around to everyone before dark. Sergeant Duane was going to stay out with the third crew, and he retained his Walkie-talkie. I had mine so we could coordinate our efforts if attacked this evening.

All of a sudden, I could hear what sounded like a C-130 flying low and coming right toward us. I shouted to the fourth squad to get ready for a drop possibly, and we needed every man ready to run out and retrieve what we could. I was briefed this could happen and we were ready. The time of day was perfect, just before the sun went completely down. The aircraft was coming directly toward us and just as it came to the edge of the tarmac, the cargo came out with only a few small chutes. Most of the supplies came out in bundles that hit and bounced and bounced again. We spent the next hour in the semidarkness collecting the goods. We were going to be in fat city from here on out with all these food supplies. I grabbed my flare pistol and let one go as a thank you. I hoped they saw it, and if they didn't, the rebels did and were probably wondering what this was all about.

Midnight arrived, and it was eerily quiet until then across the airstrip, but then the blackest darkness lit up with gunfire and then machine gun fire. I could hear grenades exploding as well. I looked over at Duane and said, "This is it Sergeant. I am going to cross the airstrip in the open and run directly in that direction. It's too slow going around and I need to be there to direct the fight. You remain here and be on the alert. Keep your Walkie-talkie at the ready, if I need anything. Let me carry a few extra bandoleers of ammo and I will get going".

Duane says, "Okay sir, and I will check the second gun position that's not that far away. These rebels may be going to try coming around looking for a weak spot to enter the airstrip." The land mass of the airstrip was sizable but not accessible on all sides due to a deep swampy area surrounding two sides of the airstrip. Growing in this swamp was nothing more than a thick underbrush no more than three feet tall. In a half dozen locations there were Congolese sentries with radio/telephone communications with Sergeant Kumba. This appeared to me as a good allocation of personnel. Sergeant Kumba knew how to stretch his men around this perimeter.

Off I went in a gallop as the battle continued. I kept moving in the right direction and had no way to alert the team I was coming. This was dangerous; however, I hoped they did not look around and notice someone coming from behind. I had my flashlight on night light, which I hoped would do if they spotted me. I arrived and got on my stomach and crawled slowly over to the MG gun emplacement. Those men surrounding the location noticed me and I got a big welcome. They explained, all was under control at the moment and I discharged my bandoleers of ammo. I called Duane.

"Alpha five this is Alpha six over, Alpha Five come in, over." When you're busy, it is best to wait a minute or two for a response before you try again. I was calling Duane, Alpha Five, and he was going to the second gun position to check on them. I waited about three minutes and no answer. "Alpha Five, Alpha Six, over." *** Alpha Five, if you are listening but can't transmit, click your receiver twice, over." Click- Click.

Now, I have a message back that tells me there is combat brewing at their location, but no actual gunfire yet. The enemy may be in their sights but no command yet to fire. This happens in combat and it is usually the enemy that is surveying the objective before commencing the battle. So we waited on the enemy. And, I waited to talk with Duane.

Pop pop! Pop, pop, pop! My walkie-talkie was live with this transmission. Duane has his mike button pressed before he talks. "Alpha Six, this is Alpha Five, over."

"Alpha Six over."

"Alpha Five here. There are a few enemy/rebels checking the security in this location. This is the action here. Our limited fire was to let them know we are here and not asleep, over."

"Alpha Six, I got it. Alpha Six Out."

The night passed with some probing gunfire in several locations along the line that the Congolese were covering. In the morning, as the sun rose, it was fairly quiet.

* * *

A week went by slowly without any assaults on the perimeter. Our afternoon siestas were fun, and with cool beer to drink we were feeling as if maybe this was the African counterpart to the Mediterranean Riviera. Evenings were quiet except for shooing off wild animals from the C ration remainders, piled up for the trash detail to remove the next day. Latrine detail had some duties as well, but we were ready for the battle when it would arrive.

Another week started and one evening, we could hear off in the distance a low-level aircraft making a pass over the airport and then swinging around and it was lined up to land. This took place just as the sun was going down. We all stood up to watch and again it was a French-looking aircraft about the size of our C-130 but sleeker in shape. It landed and pulled into the area across the airstrip. We could see the Congolese troops forming a security line around the aircraft and Sergeant Kumba could be detected with his jeep moving around in that vicinity. They were there about an hour and we wondered what they were doing, but it was none of our business. With binoculars, we could see they were unloading pallets of some kind and there were at least two dozen small pallets being stacked up.

The next day Sergeant Kumba showed up and thanked me profusely for being such a great leader/boss. He says not many Americans he knows will buy his men beer and send them C rations. I thanked him for being such a great host and allowing me to use the Jeep to go into town. Then he gave me a small parcel and cautioned me not to open it until later. It is wrapped in a paper bag with excelsior packing. I smile and wonder what it might be.

About then the plane started up and in minutes, is off the ground and there were no shots fired that I could hear. There were commercial flights that flew in once or twice a day and sometimes we could hear a few shots being fired off in the distance.

Another day passed and it was time to make another beer run. Oh, by the way, the parcel was a 9mm Browning handgun still in the anti-seize preservative. It was really nice to have this for my personal protection and I told Sergeant Kumba this as we drove off to town for more beer.

His troops were included in the purchase of beer and it cost me about $4 per case. He got 4 cases and I got 4 cases. Then we agreed to buy some type of salty crackers in the can made in Germany that were $2 per can and we bought ten cans. Candy was putrid so we bought big jars of cucumber pickles for both groups. All total my bill was about $90 US, which included a full tank of gas for the Jeep.

We passed on the barbecue simmering on the stove. It smelled good but I didn't want the troops getting sick. The other very cheap item was French rolls that were baked in the surrounding area and were very good tasting and we bought every bag on hand in the store. These went well with the C rations which contained jelly and peanut butter.

Sergeant Kumba dropped me off first and we unloaded the supplies. He saluted me and was off to tell his troops they were going to have beer for dinner. Some women from the community were providing food to the Congolese troops twice a day. I did not see what it was, but it looked like mush for breakfast and tea. Their dinner was around 2 p.m. and it was a stew of some sort. They liked their French rolls to go with that dish.

This same week around midnight when it was quiet, I could hear the movement of vehicles off in the distance and moving in our direction. I alerted the M60 gun squads when they were resting that afternoon with their beer to be on the lookout that night. Only one man per squad needed to be awake per shift and I was glad that I had reminded them not to be lazy and pay attention to what we were there for. It was only less than a week left before we were to return home, I told them.

After a few minutes of hearing these sounds of vehicles and other noises, I decided it was time to investigate. I told Sergeant Duane to turn on his Walkie-talkie and get ready for action. He was going to visit and remain with gun crew no. 2 and I was going out to gun crew no. 3, which was the most vulnerable, covering the road coming into the airport. Sergeant Kumba had a good number of his troops stationed there as well.

As I was getting ready, Sergeant Kumba showed up. He was becoming my Congolese platoon Sergeant and very attentive to my needs. He drove over to my location to get me and drive me around to all the locations. This way the two of us could cover the entire perimeter in 30 minutes. We alerted each squad of his and mine as we drove around. This was Sergeant Kumba's idea since he had no Congolese army boss. The officer in charge had left his post one night and deserted with his woman. They never saw him again.

We were all in place now and it became eerily quiet. It always seems this way just before the storm hits. At about 1:30 a.m., the fight began in one location and then another and another. Bullets were flying and we were out of the jeep and on the line helping out. A gun jeep was approaching the main entrance and my gun crew was letting them have it one short burst at a time. This fight became the fight we were hoping never to experience. These were real bullets and a few grenades thrown in. A few men, only a few of the Americans, were injured and dragged back from the line. I helped Sergeant Kumba with medical aid and then he could drive them back to the aid station he had set up.

The fight grew more intense as the night went on. There were breaks in the action, but no one was going home. One hour later I had a few men that I encountered along the line in one of the M60 gun crews who were bleeding from gunshots. Luckily they were not life-threatening and could be patched up by the medical corpsman I brought with me.

The action was continuous and the blessing was that the moon was not shining full bright. The clouds were doing the job, so we were not readily visible standing on the tarmac treating the wounded. I sent my injured men back with Kumba on the jeep, to my area aid station. This jeep was a real blessing to have and I wondered how we would get along without it.

Through the night until 4 a.m., the fight continued sporadically. As the sun began to rise and our visibility increased we could see the enemy in their civil war outfits. Mostly pieces of military clothing and little headgear except for bandannas. These native rebel fighters were supported by the then political adversary to the president of the Congo. It was a civil war and we were involved. We did discover they had good weapons made in Russia, AK47 rifles.

We had escaped what could have been a more serious scenario and we were thankful we had no death casualties. We did have a few men that were in pain from gunshot wounds, but they looked okay and the morphine was keeping them quiet and pain-free. Sergeant Kumba was the man who could go to his communication headquarters when the fighting stopped. He would give his report and request a medical evacuation of the injured from both armies. He said whoever was on duty at this location would convey his requests.

The medical evacuation chopper, a US Army Huey arrived the next morning to pick up two of my men and four of the Congolese troops. As the chopper touched down and loaded the injured, the Congolese Army pilot gave Sergeant Kumba a written note for me; addressed to the general. It was written in Congolese English which was a lot of fun translating. Basically it said thank you for saving the "night" possibly meaning winning the fight last night. Then it went on to say we Americans are the "best" and can come back again when there is no war and party with them. "Very complimentary," Sergeant Kumba told me. Then Kumba said the Airport tower operator informed him the US Air Force would be coming to pick up the Americans, tomorrow at dusk. Another group possibly a company of US infantry will be arriving on that plane. I was to leave everything including our weapons and ammo. Our only baggage was to be our backpacks.

I told Sergeant Kumba to come over in the afternoon, the next day for a beer and he agreed.

The next morning, Sergeant Duane got around to congratulate everyone on the excellent performance the night before. He told them they were combat tested, combat-ready for their tour in the infantry and would possibly receive the Combat Infantryman Badge for this action. He told them he would put a Letter of Commendation in their file for future promotion. He was proud to serve with them and they could call on him anytime they wanted advice or help.

We met with our friend Kumba who wanted to go back to the USA with us. We had made serious friends—the three of us—and our eyes watered as we drank our beer. I opened my pocket to see what was left of the money and found $250 US. I asked Sergeant Duane to check his stash. He said, "Lieutenant, General I have $150 US".

I asked Duane, "Give it to me please, and tell no one that this took place. I am giving the money left over to Sergeant Kumba and his troops for a party after we leave tonight. Okay, by you?"

"Yes Lieutenant."

"Okay, I will give this to you Sergeant Kumba for your good work and for your help to the Americans." I counted out the $400 and handed it to Kumba. He about fell over, bowing low to the ground. Bowing more to both Sergeant Duane and myself. Tears came gushing out and he was overcome with grief for us leaving and joy for knowing us. We too were emotional that Kumba would not be going with us since he was such a great person and we cared. There were handshakes and outright crying taking place.

The afternoon did not pass fast enough. We were exhausted emotionally and were ready for the extraction. Sergeant Kumba stayed with us as we loaded his jeep with all remaining beer, food and C rations. He made several trips to get it all and then stayed with us until we heard the aircraft coming.

I told Sergeant Duane to get the men ready and we waited for this aircraft to land. It was late afternoon and I wondered to myself about the rebels attacking since they could see the aircraft pretty well. I could hear a shot or two or three in the far distance but I was not that concerned.

This was a larger aircraft than the one that brought us to the Congo, I thought, and it was making its approach with enough runway ahead. The aircraft turned and we watched and waited for it to taxi to our side of the tarmac. It stopped and began to lower its ramp in the back to discharge the troops and cargo when we heard a horrible noise come from one of the four turboprop engines. As I approached the rear end to meet the new leader I heard someone yelling inside the plane, telling the troops to dismount, get out A.S.A.P. There was fire in the engine compartment and they needed to shut down the engines.

I saw the leader as he came off the aircraft and I was surprised to see he was a captain. I introduced myself to him and he immediately asked if we could help his men to deplane with all their supplies. I saluted the captain and he returned the salute and told me to hold any further recognition. Captain Flemming was his name and I called Sergeant Duane over and explained we needed our guys to help unload the plane. I would try to get Sergeant Kumba to meet the captain and help drag out the pallets.

It looked as if this group was at least ten men larger than my group.

After 30 minutes, the mission was accomplished and the plane was unloaded. Captain Flemming wanted me to call HQ and let them know that they had arrived and now there was a problem with the aircraft. I explained to the captain that we had no communication with anyone. We could go to the airstrip tower operator and ask if he could relay a message to whoever would listen and pass a message along. He was astounded by this information. He couldn't believe he was in this vulnerable position without any communication.

At this point I left and went to talk to the pilots who were inspecting the smoldering engine that they thought was hit with gunfire. They told me the aircraft could possibly take off with three engines only if there were no passengers or cargo and they would try early in the morning if that was okay. I told them it would be okay with me but when they get to their destination, they must call the Pentagon and let them know there is a platoon that needs extraction as soon as possible. Then I thought to add, and let them know that this current Army troop that just arrived could use some form of radio long-distance communications. They assured me if they made it off the ground they would comply with my request.

I spent the evening briefing Captain Flemming. I oriented and introduced him to Sergeant Kumba with the jeep. I took him around to where the machine gun emplacement crews were located along the defensive line. I explained Sergeant Kumba's delicate situation and how he liked me being his commanding officer. He called me general and I told the captain that he would probably do the same with him and not to be offended. Sergeant Kumba was a real asset in this combat situation and we should compensate him for the use of his vehicle when the Captain wanted to use it. I explained that we had a sizable expense account to buy food supplies and beverages for my men and then some for Sergeant Kumba and his men on occasion.

"Captain Wilson, you have been very helpful in your briefing to me and I want to ask you for another favor. Can you show me and the 38 men who accompanied me here, where on the line should they be located and also where are the latrines located?"

"Yes sir, but I am not a captain. I have been in the Corps for six months, but I have previous service sir. I am a second lieutenant assigned to the Second Infantry Division. My commander gave me this assignment and told me it was the most secret of anything I would be faced with and not to tell even my wife. She thinks I am in Canada on a special secret mission."

"Oh my God! I can't believe my ears. They sent you here to this location in Africa without communications and without heavy weapons. I cannot believe that they had not thought this through. This is a suicide mission in my mind, Lieutenant."

"Yes, sir, I wondered about it, but all I could do was comply with my orders. We do not have any IDs. in our possession. We had to leave our wallets and our dog tags back at Fort Benning."

"Well, what we need to do is go out with Sergeant Kumba and make the rounds with my troops. The night is approaching and if you will, Lieutenant, remain with me for your support tonight. When we can get this tribe settled, I will share with you some special supplies and drinks I brought with me. Okay by you?"

"Yes sir, I am ready when you are."

"Okay Lieutenant," Captain Flemming responded, "Let's head out."

After the men were situated on the perimeter, an hour later we were back to our makeshift campsite. Sergeant Kumba excused himself to get back to his troops. He was invited to stay awhile and have a drink, but he needed to return to his post. He thanked us and saluted us both.

Sergeant Duane had taken the initiative and put out fifty percent of our men on the line to reinforce and instruct the new troops that just arrived.

The pilots were at our campsite and were conversing with the Captain when I left to brief my men and Sergeant Duane. I told them that I would let them know when I knew anything. Until then we were going to eat C rations from the current stockpile that just arrived. I told them I would get Sergeant Kumba to bring us water for us to drink, but conserve their water until then.

I returned to the camp where the Captain was and asked if there was anything more he needed from me before I lay down for a short rest. He was busy talking and did not get my question and when I turned to go he yelled at me. "Lieutenant, aren't you going to join me for a drink?"

"No sir, I cannot drink this late before my shift. I need to be alert for whatever. But thank you very much for the offer. If the offer is still open tomorrow, I will join you. Good night, sir."

As I lay down, Sergeant Duane stopped by and said he was going to keep watch for the first five hours and would wake me at 1:00 a.m. I thanked him for his help getting everyone situated with the new troops. I told him it didn't look too promising for our getting extracted anytime soon, but to keep up the morale and we would be out of here in a few days, I hoped.

Sergeant Duane said, "Sir, I want you to know that I have appreciated your leadership and I am very fortunate to have made this weird trip with a man like you. You are very cool, sir. In the face of action you are the coolest."

"Thank you Sergeant Duane. You're pretty cool yourself. Goodnight."

* * *

I was in a deep sleep when Sergeant Duane woke me. I was for sure in a real stupor and couldn't get my bearings for at least a minute. He talked to me and said that all was quiet and peaceful. I like the sound of that, especially since I was having a hard time waking up. I think that sleep deprivation had caught up with me. I got to my feet and the sky lit up like the 4th of July. Some flares were in the air just above us and the downed aircraft. I realized it wasn't the 4th of July, so I called the front gate gun crew and told them to get ready. I believed the enemy was going to try and rush through the main gate and try and destroy the American plane. Sergeant Duane got going on a trot to gun position #3. He had his walkie-talkie with him and could communicate with the front gate since they had my walkie-talkie.

The captain rushed over to where I was standing and asked if he needed to go out to the line and I told him "No sir, we have it under control and are hoping this is just another false attack. The enemy is really good at that. They like to stir things up, but they seldom go through a full round attack."

The pilots were awake and wondering what was going on. I told them to get ready for their departure. Not this very minute, but sometime in the next hour or so depending on the level of action they should get their shit together and be ready to crank it up s soon as I give them the okay. The Captain was listening to all this and getting an ear full. He nodded to me several times, giving me his okay.

Sergeant Kumba arrived and jumped out of his jeep even before it came to a complete stop. "You need my help general?"

"Stand by Sergeant," It sounded like a few mortars exploding on the other side of the tarmac closest to the main gate. No signs of explosions on this side. Praise God! We needed to get this aircraft back home where they can make repairs. If it was damaged any further it may be an impossibility," I said out loud.

The pilots came over and told me they wanted to board the aircraft and get their pre-flight inspection completed and stand by for the GO signal. I looked over at the Captain and said, "Captain, are you in agreement that this is okay?"

Captain Flemming gave a thumbs-up signal and said he agreed this was a good choice. I agreed with his decision and told the flight crew to be careful in the dark and to be very careful with any lights, flashlights included. Don't start up anything that makes any noise. I will give you a blinking green light from my flashlight for you to get your engines started. The runway landing lights are very dim but they should be on. I will see if Sergeant Kumba can get that accomplished. Just then I sent up my signal flare for Kumba to come and the pilots departed for the aircraft with a four-man security detail leading the way.

It was now 2:45 a.m. and the battle was winding down some with our troops showing strength in numbers along the defensive line. The enemy got this message when they first started the skirmish. The volume of fire impressed them not to try anything that night. They realized they were outnumbered.

I waited about 45 minutes to see if the gunfire really was diminishing I flicked my Army night vision flashlight on green and waved it at the plane. I got a flashback of some penlight and the engines started. This was a very loud CPU generator that had to get this turboprop aircraft started. All three engines were running very satisfactory to my ear and they began to taxi. They were going to take off in the direction of the deep water swamp and not over the inhabited land to the North. With the turbines screaming away they went. It was a cooler night and the lift-off went well. They were in the air quicker than expected and we waved in the dark as they passed by.

That night seemed to mesh with the following night. There was no eventful occurrence to speak of in the interim and now we were getting very bored just sitting around. Sergeant Kumba wanted me and Sergeant Duane to come over to his side of the airstrip for dinner the next evening and we agreed. When we departed for dinner we left our senior weapons squad leader in charge.

Sergeant Kumba came for us and I told the Captain where we were going and when he could expect us to return. Okay, Lieutenant, I will keep watch while you are gone and if there is a problem I will fire a red flare into the air."

"Yes, Sir. I will keep a sharp eye out for your signal."

Kumba asked, "Do you have to ask permission to leave?"

"No, I said, I do not, but it is common courtesy to let the boss know what and where you will be."

Okay, let's have a party, a going away party!"
Exclaimed Sergeant Duane.

We did have a wonderful time and lots of good
food and beer. We ate until we could not eat
anymore. Since we had been on C rations for several
days without our beer ration we were ready for all this
good stuff. At midnight, we called it quits and
Sergeant Kumba drove us back in his jeep. We said
goodnight and he saluted us.

At 2:00 a.m., I was awakened with screaming
coming from one of my soldiers bivouacked thirty
yards away. This was excruciating screaming by one
trooper who I thought was being eaten by a tiger or
something like that. He keep it at this high pitch
until we arrived and we could see there was nothing
like what we feared. He was trying to brush off his
body a dozen African Black Army Ants about the
size of a small pumpkin seed. They were big insects
that we had not seen before but they were prevalent
in this part of Africa. They had stingers that gave you

a welt the size of a US 25-cent piece. Our trooper was in bad shape and Sergeant Kumba was contacted for help.

When Sergeant Kumba arrived he analyzed the situation and knew what to do. In the town they had a witch doctor who had a brew and a salve that he had developed over the years for this biting ant. The children in the villages were getting attacked by these aggressive ants. Sergeant Duane accompanied the trooper and Kumba to the village.

I suggested this might not be all there is to this ant infestation and so we went hunting. We discovered the colony was on the move not too distant from where we were camped. They were far enough away that we didn't need to move, but we needed to stay alert to any exploration they might do. These ants were so aggressive they could subdue animals as large as a hedgehog or large snake. In minutes the victim would be paralyzed and eaten alive.

The night went by slowly as I waited for Sergeant Kumba and Sergeant Duane to return. I heard the jeep returning and looked at my watch. It was 6 a.m. The trooper was with them and his leg was all bandaged up. They told me that the witch doctor gave him some fermented drink and then plastered his leg with a special mud that was made from hot chili peppers. Whatever it was, it was doing the job of reducing the sting and helping the trooper contend with his pain.

Another day on the strip and I was praying for this delay in our departure to be over. I wanted us to get off this detail and get on with our lives. We were tired and our attitude showed our displeasure in this mission. What were we going to do if we were left stranded here on the continent of Africa? Really now, I had a few questions from my team, about this probability. So, it was not a foreign idea. There were all kinds of ideas thrown out concerning this eventuality. I assured the troops we were going to get picked up soon; maybe a day or two more. As I said this, I too was getting anxious.

I had my C ration and a cup of coffee brought to me by the Captain. We were thankful to have this drink since we were without coffee for over three weeks. Now, we continued to wait.

Around noon Sergeant Duane came to me. "Sir, I am feeling very strange. There is something going on in my gut. It feels like there is something moving around in my stomach and then it feels like the object is trying to get into my intestines."

"Sergeant Dune, When did this first start bothering you?"

"Well, it was about two days ago that I first noticed this rumbling in my stomach. After I got back from taking Private Rawlings to the witch doctor, it really began to move around. There is something in my gut. I feel it as it moves." I reached over and put my hand on his stomach and I could feel it moving.

"Sergeant, There is only one thing to do and that is if you have no pain, then you can wait until we get back home to see the doctor. What do you think?"

"Sir, I think I can wait."

Okay, but if you begin to feel pain or nausea, you tell me and we will call in the medical team from the Congolese. But, I want you to rest and let Corporal James Thompson take over. I will call a runner out to go get him at the front gate and then he can select a replacement for himself. This is no biggie, since the other men are in charge now and we are just there for support."

"Yes, Sir, I will be in my tent if you need me."

It's the following day in the late afternoon and I see the Jeep coming quickly in our direction. Sergeant Kumba jumps out of his vehicle and yells out to me, "Sir general, I have good news for you. The airport tower guy gave me a message he got over his radio for you. Be on the lookout tomorrow evening for your pickup."

"This is good news, Sergeant. I was wondering if we are ever going to get out of here. We will miss you and if you are ever in America you can look us up in Colorado. Okay?

"Yes sir lieutenant general. I am going to try to come see you and then we can make a meeting with the boss for me to join the American army."

"That sounds good to me Sergeant. If you make it to America before I get out of the army it will be easy for you to find me. But, if it is later than two years, you will need to come to Colorado and find me. You understand?"

Sergeant Kumba asked about Sergeant Duane and I told him he was sick in his stomach. He was resting in his tent and Kumba wanted to see him before he departed. I told him to go ahead and visit him in his tent.

* * *

Sometime later as I was wandering around the area I ran into the Captain. I said, "Captain, Can I talk with you sir?

"Yes certainly, what's up?"

"Well Sir, I just got notice from the tower, a message that there will be an aircraft tomorrow evening arriving to extract us."

"Well, it's about time you get out of this hole. You know this was just a bump in your career. Never will you see anything about this mission that you accepted for the President. In other words you will never mention it since it a classified secret and you will never hear a word mentioned about it from the Pentagon. Not even a thank you will come to any of you for your help here in the Congo. I can assure you of that since my briefing was very complete by my commanding general at Fort McClellan in Virginia. Got it."

"Yes sir, I got it. No one will ever know about this except the men in my platoon and you sir. When you become a general I would like you to remember our platoon when you write the commendation for your men involved in this mission. I think all the men deserve the commendation when you write it up sir. I will be over shortly to have a farewell snort with you."

Okay, I will see you soon."

When I told Sergeant Duane we were going to be picked up; he was excited.

I told him to get the word out to the men to get their shit together and be sure the area was clean as they found it and no trash to be found anywhere in this area. I told him there would be an exit meeting tomorrow after evening chow. This was going to be a very important meeting that everyone will attend. He agreed to get the word out and would check with me later tonight about a few things.

Cocktails with the Captain were always good. He must have brought with him a footlocker full of booze. The only things he needed were limes and lemons and ice to complete his bar. These items he scrounged with Sergeant Kumba's help. He was learning how helpful Sergeant Kumba could be and I encouraged him to be friends with the Sergeant. I asked him if there was a way to get Sergeant Kumba out of Africa with his wife. He looked at me very strange and did not answer.

The morning came and it was our last day in the Congo. The men were mentally relaxed and ready for their departure. They were busy with their work getting the area picked clean of anything not natural to the area and it was looking normal again. I wanted to leave a good impression for the other soldiers to see.

I couldn't get excited about our departure for some reason. I told Sergeant Duane I was not in the best mindset for this day and he should stay on the alert for whatever was to come. "Sergeant Duane, I will be here in my tent resting for a while. My mind is not at rest and I will tell you later what is going on. Okay?"

I was struggling with the decision of what to do with the pistol given to me by Sergeant Kumba as a present. It was not a big problem, but it was contraband and it was not official equipment that I could testify was mine. It was unofficially mine to use while I was at the airport, but not to take back to the USA. There were principles to follow when in a foreign land and engaged in combat. You were not to confiscate anything for your own personal equipment or use. This is not a rule, but is common sense not to steal. This item would be called into question if any other problem came into play. So, I needed to leave the pistol here in Africa and take no mementos of this operation, not even a bottle cap.

Dinner arrived in Sergeant Kumba's jeep. It was the stew meat concoction we had to learn to eat and rolls which we loved. He must have spent all the money we gave him for this feast, which included some fruit, soda and chocolate-like candy. Kumba was so excited to see how we liked his food and how we showed our appreciation by shaking his hand over and over again. Each man stood up and thanked Sergeant Kumba for his help and for his friendship. They even showed a little emotion some of the time as they said their goodbyes.

As the sun went down, Sergeant Kumba stayed with us. He lingered among the troops, telling them how much he wanted to become one of them. He was sad he was not going to America with them but wanted to stay in touch. He was handing out a shortwave radio address that might work. The tower operators at the airport had a shortwave radio in the tower that at times, could pick up messages. So he was telling his friends to send him messages.

The evening was quiet except for the animals and birds that hung around, as well as insects of every kind that made noises. So there were background noises, but no gunfire that I could hear. It was lovely thinking about our going home tonight. Twenty nine days of Africa was enough for me. It was right then I had a thought that my army career as a rifle platoon leader was not going to last long if I was going to go on missions like this. I had learned, however that you can get killed by ignorant superiors. As the Captain said, they sent me and my platoon out here to be massacred. We had no communications and no backup if we got into real trouble. Wow! That was behind us now and we were just waiting.

Dusk turned to night and there was no aircraft. At about 10 p.m., we heard the liberating sound of an aircraft coming and then we saw the very limited runway lights turn on. The sound came from some distance but we knew it was a low slow flight approach. Then the aircraft lights came on just as they were about to touch down and it was a perfect landing.

Sergeant Kumba was there and as I came over to him, he was crying. He was very upset he was not going. I assured him we would see him again in America. Then I gave him the pistol and told him I could not bring it back to America. I told him to give it to the Captain and tell him it is a present from you and don't tell him you gave it to me first. He will be very much liking it and it will bring good luck to Kumba. He thanked me for the advice and told me he would never forget this time in his life. I agreed and followed the troops and Sergeant Duane out to the aircraft. The crew chief had everything under control and we were loaded in minutes.

We made it home after departing the flight in Miami and reloading a flight to Atlanta and then a bus ride to Columbus. It took three days to arrive home to our waiting families. I'm sorry to say, there was no honor guard or band playing on our arrival.

FISHING OFFSHORE IN THE SEA OF JAPAN

It was 4 a.m. and totally dark as my brother and I catapulted down the track. The temperature was cool and the Japanese commuter train was rocking and rolling back and forth. The train jerked uncontrollably because of the uneven track and with such force, I suspected it could derail. Most trains of this early age were a rough ride, but this was probably one of the roughest.

We were headed south on the train to Odawara, a small fishing village on the East coast of Japan about 50 miles south of Yokohama. What was noticeably different was at this time of morning, the train was empty except for the conductor. We were finally going deep-sea fishing with our friend, Mrs. Hara, who promised us this trip. She was going to introduce my brother and I, who were high schoolers, to her uncle for this event. He was a licensed commercial fisherman and he had consented to take all of us fishing.

Our anticipation showed by our continual question to Mrs. Hara, "How much farther?" Mrs. Hara's answer was only her oriental grin and she continued looking out the window.

My head and neck felt like I had just finished a Sumo wrestling match. It was sore already with the jerking and jostling motion of the train. I experienced some vertigo and nausea because of this and looked to see how the others were doing. They looked fine and the train picked up more speed on its way south. The faster it went, the worse the ride. We were about forty-five minutes out of Yokohama before the train started slowing down. As I looked out the window, there was nothing much to see. It was dark and what I could make out were giant sand dunes shining in the moonlight. Finally, the conductor motioned for us to get ready at the exit for our dismount and departure. I balked at this command and looked at Mrs. Hara. She nodded it was okay and we took three stairs down and jumped into the sand when the train stopped. It was much colder that time of the morning than I had expected. The cool breeze from the ocean was partially responsible and I could hear the surf at some distance but could not see it. It was strange standing in the sand in the dark and wondering what we were doing in the middle of the Sahara sand dunes. Just as I was about to ask which way to go, Mrs. Hara, her two daughters and sons took off toward the beach.

My brother, Rick looked around and motioned to me. "What do you think?" I looked around and said, "We got no choice, follow her, she knows the way."

This all came about in the summer of 1954 when my father, an Army officer of twenty-plus years, was transferred to Japan after serving 13 months in the Korean conflict. He had been second in command as a lieutenant colonel to a Korean general, Park, who commanded a small detachment of soldiers who were trained to interrogate prisoners. Dad was decorated with the Silver Star for his performance and assigned to Japan for his next tour. My brother and I were living in Georgia at the time and Dad requested we join him in Japan.

We were excited to see our dad and especially excited to be heading for another foreign land we could explore. We packed; Mother put the household goods in storage and we headed for San Francisco. It didn't take us long, possibly ten days at sea, with a stop in Honolulu before arriving in Yokohama. While our dad loved his boys, he was not very expressive, and yet we were always eager to hug and kiss him when we greeted each other after these separations. He picked us up at the Yokohama pier, dressed impeccably and looking very military, as always. We were very happy to see him again after almost two years. Each of us embraced him with hugs and kisses while we held him close. Dad had his own unique, sweet smell that made me feel safe in his arms. Back in Georgia, I was worried that I might not see my father again except to attend his funeral. I was very happy to have been proven wrong.

We had a great reunion on the pier. Dad suggested he take us to dinner before we returned to his quarters in Yokohama Engineering Depot (Y.E.D.). We stopped at the Yokohama Officers Club for dinner and celebrated with all kinds of excellent shrimp and crab dishes. Mom was letting us boys do a lot of the talking since we were so excited but the minute they brought out the food, our attention shifted to the innumerable delicacies in front of us. Mom was not looking so well, so Dad asked her how she was feeling. She said she would talk to him about it later since we were all having such a good time.

After dinner, he drove us to Y.E.D, some forty miles inland, where he was the executive officer. Yokohama Engineering Depot was a large facility that was the station where all the used and damaged military equipment and vehicles found around the Pacific area were being collected and dismantled for export back to the States.

We stayed a few days at the officer's billets before he took us to the house he had rented in the town of Hashimoto, a little farming town about ten miles away, which was going to be our new home.

One of Dad's friends at the Depot told him about Mrs. Hara, who leased out her guesthouse to Americans. He had met with her and had contracted a lease for the summer. We were going to stay in her cottage, Dad told us. My mother, under duress, went to the hospital to rest under her doctor's care the day after we arrived. The building stress of the past couple of years, being alone and not knowing if Dad would return from the war, had taken a great toll on her. Mom was completely worn out emotionally. Getting ready for our trip and taking care of all the household and travel details, my mother had depleted her remaining energy and was now experiencing a not-too-critical nervous breakdown. The doctors recommended to my father that my mother needed a short rest away from all the humdrum of life.

We moved our suitcases into this very nice western-style cottage. It truly was built as a honeymoon cottage by the previous owners, and Mrs. Hara had been renting it out since her husband died. The three of us would be living there for the next couple of months while our mother recuperated in the hospital. Dad would go to work in the morning, and Rick and I would spend the day with the Hara family, which we enjoyed immensely.

The Hara family comprised Mrs. Hara, her four children and her husband's mother. Her two boys were about the same age as my brother and me.

Yoichi was just starting his first year at Toyo University and I was a senior in high school, while Tetsugi, his brother, was a year younger than me. We all hit it off and were the best of buddies in just a matter of days. The daughters, Kayoko and Sumiko, were younger, very quiet and stayed mostly in the background. Mrs. Hara, who was educated in China by American missionaries, spoke fluent English. She was very friendly and entertained us boys with some type of activity every day. We were together most of the days and ate many of our meals with them when our father was away at work.

Dad brought us news about Mother when he returned from the hospital each evening. She was improving and regaining her energy, he said. We did get to see her on weekends and felt she was getting better, as well. She anticipated she would be out in a couple of weeks, so we planned to celebrate with her when that day arrived. We could see she had lost weight but we knew how to remedy that when she got out. The three of us were the best short-order cooks around and could fatten her up quickly.

I relayed the message from Mrs. Hara about how she was eager to meet our mother and wanted her to get well quickly. Mrs. Hara was truly concerned about Mom and told us she would improve more quickly if she was with us at home. While we agreed with her, we told her the doctors wanted her in the hospital instead.

Meanwhile, Mrs. Hara started us on a course in conversational Japanese. This kept us occupied for several hours each day. In addition to language training, we played baseball in their backyard. A miniature form of lot ball kept us busy on the days we were not on safari. Most days, we were out traveling on the train, visiting neighboring towns, shopping, or just visiting Mrs. Hara's friends. She was so proud of us and wanted to show us off to all her friends and relatives. Whatever her agenda, we always had a good time.

On several occasions, we asked her if she could take us deep-sea fishing. My brother and I loved to fish and had many memories of deep-sea fishing in Georgia and Florida. She said she would need to see if one of her uncles would invite us to go fishing with him. One was a deep-sea fisherman and we would have to go with him if we were going. There was no deep-sea sport fishing available in northern Japan that she knew about. Therefore, she explained if we wanted to go fishing, we had to go out with a licensed fisherman. We thought about it for a second; worried the offer would be retracted, I looked at my brother and we exclaimed, "Okay!"

While we waited for her uncle's answer, we continued to explore the countryside and played baseball and Mahjong. Mahjong was a game very popular in Japan and all the kids and many adults played it. It was similar to dominos and gin rummy combined, played with little domino-like ivory blocks. You did keep score and if you were gambling, then it got even more exciting. Yoichi had friends from college he would invite over for the weekend to play. Let me tell you, the game started on Friday evening after a fantastic meal of Sukiyaki and rice wine to drink. Then we boys would go up stairs to Yoichi and Tetsugi's room to play. Only four could play at a time and the others would read, listen to music or sleep until it was their turn. Mrs. Hara would bring tea and cookies up to the room every few hours to keep us going. This game would continue nonstop until midnight Sunday. Everyone would count up their points and then say their goodbyes before they headed for the train station. Yoichi's friends all lived in the Tokyo area closer to their school so they had an hour train ride home. This was what I called marathon Mahjong and it was a whole lot of fun. We sometimes played it with the family, but not often. It seemed to be a boy's game mostly and the girls appeared shy and uninterested in playing.

It wasn't too long after one of these Mahjong marathons that Mrs. Hara told us she had heard from her uncle and we were going fishing. Mrs. Hara planned the day and the snacks and lunch to take with us. My dad got briefed and Mrs. Hara assured him we would all be careful. Her uncle was an experienced fisherman and we should be in good hands, she told him. We were excited when Dad agreed we could go. "You boys need to be careful on this trip and watch out for Mrs. Hara and her family. They may not be able to swim and it would be tragic if anything happened to them. Promise me you will be wise and not get into any trouble. I do not want your mother to be worried," he said to us before we left. Mrs. Hara was sketchy with the details because she didn't know any. We had to wait until we got there to find out what kind of fish we were going to catch. I also wondered what kind of fishing gear we were going to use.

Finally, the day arrived. Mrs. Hara told us to set our clocks for 3 a.m. We would be getting on the train at 3:45 at the Hashimoto station and then transfer at Sagami Ono (Sagami station) to the train that went south along the coast to Odawara. We hadn't traveled more than a half hour when the conductor came and spoke to Mrs. Hara. She told us we were almost there. The train stopped with a jerk and it was still pitch black outside. Mrs. Hara went to the exit door to help the girls off the train and then directed us guys to jump down. I originally thought we were getting off at a station, so I was surprised that we had just dismounted somewhere along the tracks with sand dunes rising up all around us.

Now I yelled to Mrs. Hara, "Where are we?" We were surely in the Sahara desert with this much sand. Mrs. Hara waved her arm and signaled for us to follow her. We were standing ankle-deep in the sand as the train pulled away. It was very dark except for the stars and the moon, throwing dim light on us and the dunes. No other light was visible anywhere. I said to Rick, "I wonder if this was a mistake and we have somehow invaded the movie set of Lawrence of Arabia." Rick laughed and told me to get a move on.

In the darkness, Mrs. Hara stumbled across the tracks and up the dune. I knew we were close to the beach when I could hear the ocean surf, yet only the dunes were in sight. We were headed in the right direction and as we gained the crest of this giant dune, we could finally see the ocean and the surf breaking onto the shore below us. I also could make out an army of men scurrying around on the beach. There was a humongous bonfire going, with many standing around warming themselves and talking. I also noticed two large Viking-style wooden hull boats parked on the beach. From this distance, it was hard to make out the details.

As we started slipping and sliding down the dune toward the beach, it all came into focus. The men we were watching were short, around five feet tall and broad-shouldered with very little clothing on. Some were wearing shorts and others had a breechcloth wrapped around their groin. They all had large, colorful bandanas around their heads and we could see their broad shoulder muscles clearly in the firelight. These men were seriously tanned, almost black, from working continuously in the sun. They looked more African or Indian than Japanese.

The big question was how we were going to fish and where was Mrs. Hara's uncle. I was having some doubts that we were actually going fishing. Mrs. Hara explained on board the train that these men were commercial tuna fishermen and we would be going commercial tuna fishing. I wondered what I had gotten us into and rolled my eyes at my brother Rick. He smiled again, knowing what I was thinking. "Bill," he called out in the dark, "this is going to be a real experience. Did you know that we are going to watch these guys' fish? I thought you said we were going fishing." He didn't understand it either. All we could do now was wait and see.

A little while later, we could see the sun rising up on the horizon and we got our bearings. Looking down the beach a mile, I could see two fishing trawlers coming in our direction. This seemed to get everyone excited and the men began to roll the two forty-foot Viking-style net boats into the surf. These two boats were piled high with nets and appeared to be linked together. We were watching a monumental feat with about sixty or seventy men chanting as they pushed the boats into the surf. Several of the men with long wooden poles standing on top of the nets continued pushing the boats into deeper water. As the trawlers came close, they linked up one net boat to each trawler and everyone scrambled aboard the net boats. We were transported in a motorized dinghy almost too small for the seven of us to one of the trawlers or powerboats, as I will call them. Once we were on board, they headed out into the open ocean, powerboats in front with net boats pulled behind. So this was our fate; trapped on a tuna trawler, we would plow the ocean waves for a day's catch.

This was different and not my idea of deep-sea fishing. Here we were, the entire Hara family, Rick and I, on the deck of a powerboat. As we headed out to sea, we talked among ourselves and I asked Mrs. Hara, "This is not what we thought you meant when you said we were going fishing. Is there any chance we can get off this boat and go home?"

"I do not think it is possible to get off the boat," she said.

"Well, we are not too happy with this situation," I told her. She explained she didn't really know what to expect herself since she did not get any briefing. All our questions, if we had any, were communicated to Mrs. Hara and she would try asking one of the crewmen. The crew was so busy they did not have time to talk. Mrs. Hara did get a chance to ask one of them where we were going and how long we would be on this trip. The only upside was that the weather was a little overcast, which kept it cooler than we expected and the surf was moderately calm. So, we decided to make the best of it.

As we got offshore ten miles or more, we lost sight of land. Shading our eyes, we began to see several small motorized boats in the distance. One of the crew finally came to Mrs. Hara and explained what was happening. These small motorized boats had a box-like seat mounted on the end of an upright pole that stood eight feet in the air. A person would climb the pole and set down in this cat box seat. These men were called scouts and their job was to find the tuna and with binoculars and red signal flags, they would direct the powerboats to where they could see the tuna feeding. When they spotted a school of tuna, they would send signals with their flags where the tuna were located. I asked how they could see where the tuna were feeding. The crewman began to explain as he pointed to the spot where we were headed.

Since the signaling, we were now plowing through the waves at full power and the crewman told us to watch the sea birds. When we saw the sea birds diving into the water, that is where the tuna were feeding, we were told. He said, the small fish or sardines that were only four to eight inches long were pushed to the surface by the tuna, which would rush up from below and catch as many as they could in one pass. This was quite a commotion with fish jumping all over the place and the gulls, pelicans and cormorants diving into the water to get their share. It was a sight to see with hundreds of birds crash-diving into the sea after the sardines. The smaller fish were jumping out of the water to escape and the water boiled with this activity. This was a scene that needed filming for National Geographic, but never a camera is available when you need one.

The powerboats were plowing through the waves like two steam locomotives plowing snow from the tracks. Side by side, they plowed ahead, then split apart, each pulling a net boat behind. As this happened, I noticed what looked like a large six-foot-diameter glass cork being tossed into the water. Tied to it was the beginning of the net that the crewmen began to toss overboard. Each net boat going in the opposite direction was dumping the net into the water as fast as they could. After a few minutes, we could see that the powerboats were making a giant circle almost a quarter mile in diameter. Each net boat had about thirty men standing on top as they unfolded the net and pushed it off into the water. The crewman explained that the net only hung down twenty-five feet from the surface and the net boat crewman had to close the bottom of the net once the fish were totally surrounded. What they did when the net boats completed their circle was to try and close the bottom of the net before the fish knew what was happening. If they detected anything, they would dive under the net and get away. You see, the crew had to work quickly to pull the rope that was woven to the bottom of the net. This operation pulled the net closed. It was like trying to catch a gold fish in an aquarium by cupping your hands together under the fish. Your hands, in this case, are the net. This whole procedure can easily take an hour to surround the fish and close the net. We listened carefully to the men as they chanted together while they pulled the rope. It was not an easy task and to stay in sync, they chanted "heave ho" or something to that effect in Japanese. It was pleasurable hearing them sing their chant. When they had the rope pulled in and the net tightly shut, they took a break from the exhaustive work. They looked intently for any signs they had made a catch. Now they must begin pulling all the net out of the water back into the two net boats. As they pulled and stacked the net, we could not see any signs of fish. They had missed this catch.

Talking with one of the crewmen, he explained that this was the routine and it could go on like this several times before they would catch anything. Wow, what a lot of work to catch a tuna, I thought, and away we went under full power. Again, there was more commotion as the scouts indicated another feeding frenzy on the surface a mile or so away. The flags were waving and we began flying through the surf at full speed, heading for the spot where we could see the birds circling and diving into the water. The tuna were again coming from below to catch their dinner on the surface. This time, the crew seemed more in earnest and it was quieter among them as they dumped the net into the water. It took another hour or more to pull in the net and again, the same thing happened. The leader of each of these schools of tuna was smarter than their hunters and when they detected danger, they would dive to avoid the danger. In each case, it is the net that frightens them.

All day, this went on with as many as five or six passes and everyone was exhausted, including Mrs. Hara and her girls. Her boys were doing okay and all of us were lightly snacking on food Mrs. Hara had packed for lunch. The sun was a scorcher and after six hours at sea, the coastal breeze and burning sun had taken its toll. My throat was swollen shut for lack of moisture and I was weary from all this activity. I didn't eat much due to the surf and my slightly upset stomach, so I began to feel the stress of the day.

This excursion was my fault and I had enough of this nonsense. No way was I ever going to ask to go deep-sea fishing again—in Japan. What had inspired me to want to do this anyway? I thought maybe it would be fun to catch a few groupers or sea bass and have a fish fry with the Haras, but this wasn't any fun. Now they were shouting again and pointing in another direction. It was almost dusk and the sun was going down. It must have been seven p.m. or later and I hadn't seen land all day. I began to wonder where we were and if these guys knew it was getting dark. If we started this routine again this late, we wouldn't be home for another three to four hours. I explained this to Mrs. Hara and she looked extremely tired and maybe even a little sea sick. She nodded her head without speaking and I could see she was not well. We guys seemed to be doing okay so far, maybe a little thirsty.

I had to admit I was becoming slightly more motivated for these fishermen to make a catch. I positioned myself at the bow up front so I could see exactly where we were going and I wondered, "Where to now?" From my vantage point, I was getting indications that I knew what these scouts were signaling and where they wanted us to drop the nets. With as much practice, I bet I could have taken over at this juncture and done a decent job directing this operation. They were moving as fast as these powerboats would go and the breeze felt good on my face. I looked over the swells at the other powerboat and about then, they began to steer away from each other. The buoy was again tossed out and the net began to tumble into the sea. This circle seemed bigger than those before. I assumed it must be an optical illusion that takes place in the fading light of dusk. All objects seem much bigger when the sunsets and the remaining light grows dimmer.

Finally, the net was closed and the anticipation was killing me. Did we do it or not? Were there any fish in the net or were we skunked again? What was the answer? I was anxious and couldn't stand it a moment longer. It was so eerie quiet as everyone stared into the dark water. There was a single yell and some Japanese words, Hiyaku! And then several yells and still more excitement as more of the crew began yelling they had caught a whole school of tuna. Actually, I got the word it was a really good catch, but I still was not able to see the fish. I was excited for them. I knew it was not good to return empty-handed, especially after ten or eleven hours of work. All of a sudden, there was another commotion and the crew ran to the bow where I was standing and pointed and yelled, "There it is!"

There, what is? I wondered. There was something big, long and black swimming very fast in the net. It was a swordfish about ten feet long with a pointed bill three feet long coming out its nose. It was a terrifying moment for us all. This giant monster fish was threatening the entire fishing operation and us. This was a dangerous situation for the fisherman. If this swordfish desired, it could bust through the net and all the tuna would be lost. They had to stop this giant fish from destroying the net and letting all the fish go. A small dingy was immediately lowered into the water with a crewman and as he pushed away from the powerboat, I could see he had a harpoon in his hand. They explained to Mrs. Hara that he must harpoon this fish if they were to have any tuna to take home. This was very dangerous to do since it was a fast-moving target and many crewmen had been hurt trying this stunt.

Swish, it passed again and you could see, even in the dark, this creature flying by just under the surface. It was huge and scaring all the tuna fish. The tuna caught were about two to four feet long, jumping totally out of the water to get away from this menace. The harpooner raised his harpoon in the ready position and thrust it down into the deep. It hit the fish and blood filled the water around it. It was a direct hit and blood gushed out all over the water. He pulled it to the side of the dingy and then we could see it more clearly. It was a large swordfish much longer than the dingy itself, probably twelve feet long. With the giant fish captured, it was now safe again to continue pulling in the net. "Heave Ho," they chanted until the tuna fish were flopping around on the surface. It was a big catch, maybe a hundred or more big tuna, twenty to fifty pounds each. They gathered them easily with their gaffs and put them into the waiting hold where they had early this morning stored lots of ice. These fish would be taken to the factory tonight and processed within hours after they arrived back home. These were the famous Pacific Blue-Fin tuna and they were a pretty sight.

As we began our journey home, the mood of the fisherman was totally different. They were joyous for the catch and sitting on the net piled high, they quietly rested. This was a very strenuous day, and luckily, it had been profitable. We were as tired as they were and all we did was watch. We hadn't pulled the rope or the net. My back was hurting just from a sympathetic reaction and I sat there on the gunnels, parched, watching for land. How far out had we been? Finally I began to see lights and see what looked like the entire island of Japan. These seafaring pilots who were born to search the sea and make their living from it never got lost. These seafarers were like the gulls that could be blown out to sea for hundreds of miles and like homing pigeons to find their way back. We continued in one specific direction until I could see those same fires burning on the beach again. What a relief we had made it back safe and sound!

It wasn't over yet, even though we were ready to depart. They came and picked us up and delivered us to the beach. It was almost midnight and in the dark, what we saw was a long line of women and some teenagers, maybe seventy or eighty, coming in single file down the beach with baskets on their heads. They marched up to the net boat and the crewman handed down a large tuna for the person to carry in their basket. When they had the fish secure in the basket, they put them on their heads and started walking slowly up the beach to a waiting vehicle for delivery to the cannery.

While this was going on, Mrs. Hara's uncle came to where we were standing and escorted us to a spot on the crest of the sand dune where a few chairs and stools were arranged. In the middle of nowhere, here was a little field kitchen set up to clean fish. They had several small tuna around twenty inches long laid out on the wooden crate and the chef or crewman was sharpening his knife. We were told to sit down for a cup of tea and we watched the man fillet the fish in small pieces. He put it on a bamboo tray with some green mustard and it was passed around. Each of us was expected to sample the catch, which I later learned was part of their custom. Raw fish or Sushi turned out to be very good even though the ladies did not eat any. Brother Rick and I dug in and had several pieces. They were even tastier, doctored with soy sauce and green mustard.

When we were finished, we all stood and did what good Japanese guests do. We bowed and bowed some more, all the while thanking Mrs. Hara's uncle. Domoaligato gozimus! Or thank you very much, which we repeated many times. He stopped to ask Mrs. Hara if we wanted some of the swordfish. Now we were hauling two big chunks of swordfish they had wrapped very nicely for us to carry on the train. The only problem we recognized was that with everything else we had to carry, we were burdened with this smelly fish. All the way home, we grumbled about the weight of these two packages.

When we finally arrived home, Dad was awake and concerned about where we had been. He said he wondered if a big fish had eaten us or something like that had happened. Mrs. Hara assured him we had no control over these wild fishermen and we were lucky they did get their catch, or we might still be on the ocean searching for tuna. We said our good nights and headed for bed after we put the swordfish in the refrigerator.

In the morning, we recounted the whole story to our father for his enjoyment. He wanted to know about the swordfish and we told him that we would prepare a few swordfish steaks for his dinner when he returned from work that evening. He agreed this was a good idea and we spent the day butchering the fish into small pieces for cooking on the grill. Mrs. Hara had never cooked swordfish, so we were on our own, she said, but we could use her knives to fillet this fish.

When Mother was briefed by Dad the next day about our activities, she almost fainted. She demanded the doctor let her go before her family destroyed themselves—and she was serious. Dad was able to smooth over the details and assure her of our faithfulness to be safe. We promised we would not try anything again without her approval. A few weeks later, she left the hospital and rejoined us at the cottage.

We recounted all the activities of the day before and marveled at the way these men made their living as part of a fishing cooperative. We had learned that each man was a partner in the operation and derived most of his support from fishing, with only a little farming to fill in. These men had been fishermen from early youth, but the tradition was changing. Due to new methods of harvesting tuna, these men would be out of a job in just a few years and that was difficult to think about. What would these skilled hunters do when their world of fishing came to an end? These proud men of the sea fearlessly making their livelihood from the notorious Sea of Japan would fade away. Never again would these lives be in contention with Mother Nature for their support. Soon, the end would come and this way of life would be over.

This was an exciting adventure and a fishing trip, never to be matched. It remains a truly fascinating story told over and over and now, more than fifty years later, it is still vivid in my memory.

1ˢᵗ CALVARY DIVISION
PLEIKU HIGHLANDS
VIETNAM 1965

Capt. Stone, company commander of A Co., acting as Alpha Six. "Alpha Six this is Red Team Six over".

"Alpha Six go ahead Red Team Six, over"

"Roger Alpha Six, lifting off 10:30 for LZ Drop Off, over".

"Alpha Six, roger out."

This is a story of a reaction force called the Red Team. At one juncture, the 1st Brigade of the 8th Cavalry's search and destroy operation included security when the enemy was attacking civilians along Highway 19 in the Highlands near the town of Pleiku. These Rebels (civilian sympathizers) were robbing anyone on the highway when they had the opportunity.

Piasters, Vietnamese money, were especially high on the list of bounty and if they paid them, usually there was no harm done to these civilian vehicle owners. You could not predict where these rebels would show up next. Our tactical operations command, TOC, came up with an idea to confront and destroy these rebels and sometimes regulars. This project was called the Red Team. A platoon of infantry soldiers 20 plus strong would be on alert standing by at a landing zone (LZ) for quick deployment. The concept was for the stand-by platoon to be ready to depart to any location in the shortest amount of time and surprise the enemy. This meant one platoon was on call for a period of days and the 1st Platoon of A Company was placed on this stand-by detail.

The highlands of Vietnam are beautiful, pristine-looking, untouched by humans. If you have seen the Ethiopian Highlands in Africa, you recall untouched fields of waist-high grass and acacia trees as far as the eye could see. This was the view but not as expansive a view as on the African continent. The ground is soft and felt like compacted sawdust, spongy-like. It was reddish in color and felt strange to walk on. This condition in the highlands was unusual since the remainder of the country was relatively forested, with some jungle and thick underbrush, and along the coast, it looked like any other South Pacific country with beautiful beaches and coconut palms. Here in the Highlands, it was quite different and the elevation was not more than two thousand feet above sea level.

The 1st platoon, designated the Red Team, was called to stand by for pickup. "Red Team Six, this is Alpha Six, proceed to LZ for extraction. Over"

"Roger, Red Team Six, out."

I was the first lieutenant in charge and was briefed on where we were going. The trouble along Highway 19 was that the traffic was blocked. Four Huey aircraft were on their way to pick up the platoon. This way, it would be just minutes before these men could get to their destination. Many times, this quick response would shock the enemy. These were identified as civilian sympathizers dressed in black pajamas and straw hats. Sometimes, they were called Viet Cong and may have been indoctrinated, but these people were not well trained and were, to my knowledge, mostly rebels with limited weapons.

We could hear the choppers coming. Their noise is distinctive, chop, chop, chop and Swoosh sounds as they landed all four, kicking up a cloud of dust on the LZ at the Tea Plantation. The men loaded and these whirly birds lifted off in less than 40 seconds.

We flew across the landscape just barely above the tree tops. Ten minutes later, we touched down in an open field with chest-high grass. I warned the guys to look out for Punjabi stakes that were ideal weapons for this tall grass.

It's a touch-and-go landing, which means the men have seconds to get off the chopper. We had to get our bearings once on the ground and with help from the platoon sergeant, we checked for due north before we set our direction and headed toward the highway 3/4 mile away.

These infantry soldiers were young guys with no experience. The platoon sergeant and platoon leader had a little. Age-wise, the platoon sergeant was just 40 with prior military experience and the platoon leader was in his late twenties also with prior military experience. Age was not necessarily a factor, but experience was important.

The platoon formed up in a single file, with the platoon leader in the middle and the platoon sergeant taking up the rear of the column. There were approximately 4 to 5 paces between the men. The platoon was strung out and looked like a giant anaconda weaving through the tall grass. The point man was a Native American recruit who was just a few years older than most of the others. He had a good sense about him and was almost always the guy out in front. He could sense anything abnormal that would tip him off to some activity looming ahead. When his arm raised high, the whole column stopped. Wait, listen, listen some more, and then he would wave us on when the coast was clear. The grass was chest-high and looking carefully, I did not see where the grass had been disturbed. We were heading in the direction of Highway 19 and at times, when stopped, we thought we could hear faint voices off in the distance in the direction we were traveling. Moving slowly and stealthily without a sound, there was off on my right, about five yards away, a mighty blood-curdling roar! Every foot locked in place and every head turned to see what it was.

It was the roar of a tiger, a Bengal tiger that inhabited South and North Vietnam. In that second, when the tiger roared, he was expressing his frustration and anger for us disturbing him. He did not charge us fortunately. Half of the platoon had passed by not seeing him in the tall grass and he was okay with that. The continual movement of troops filing by finally upset him. He jumped up from his position on his belly where he had been eating his meal. When I observed his position, I saw the remains of half a carcass of a wild pig. This meant we had intruded on his kill.

Now was not the time to discuss what had just happened. I, the platoon leader, was truly the closest to the tiger; he was full-grown and probably weighed easily 300 or more pounds. This is one of the areas of the world that is a habitat for Bengal tigers. If there had not been this whole file of men coming so close to him, he would probably have attacked, but our numbers overwhelmed him. We continued in file for another hundred yards before we stopped again. Not a word was spoken, not a sound made through all of this, and my heart was pounding out of my chest. Still in file, we continued in the direction of the sounds we heard in the distance.

As we approached, we hunkered down. We could see several individuals with weapons in front of a truck holding back the traffic and I waved to the squad leaders to go left and to go right so that we were in a line facing the road. The platoon moved into position and I instructed only one man to fire his weapon. This way, we had the element of surprise and could see what the enemy would do. We could not identify how many there were, but there were at least a dozen vehicles stopped. We received a return volley and that was it. Only one volley in our direction and they were gone. When we rushed over to the road, the rebels departed into the thickest of the grass, heading for the river. We did not follow.

After talking with the driver of the truck, who understood a little English, he told me these rebels were trying to extort money from them. Those in this vehicle convoy had been stalling with any payment and hoping someone would come along to rescue them.

"Alpha Six this is Red Team Leader over".

"Red Team Leader, mission complete, ready for pickup at LZ Drop Off, over."

"Roger that, Alpha Six out."

We hustled our way back to the spot closest to where we were dropped off.

Now there was something to talk about later that day and how we might have had a tiger pelt to bring back with us. We also asked about other animals in the area we should know about, including the elephants seen a month ago. We had heard a few stories about monkeys, snakes and other dangerous insects like scorpions. But nobody told us to watch out for tigers!

A few weeks later, after the Red Team experience, the platoon was in the highlands again close to Pleiku City. There had been, for many years, a French family who owned a tea plantation and had built a small runway for their plane. It was a good place to bivouac and for the choppers to pick up troops. Because there was a hard top to the runway, which helped keep the dust down. The platoon was spread out around one end of the landing strip and was on duty for security at night but was there waiting for a call to reinforce another company if needed. During the nights, only 30% were on the alert at one time and so the troops alternated being on guard through the night. It was a three-hour shift, so each shift had time to sleep.

One night, I awoke to relieve myself and as I stepped around several sleeping troops to find a location to urinate. I notice something on the ground race by me. Shadows in the night are always alarming if you do not know what they are. I waited for the shadow to return but after a few minutes, I returned to my position. There would be time in the morning to research what I saw in the moonlight.

As dawn approached, I was up as the Battalion mess arrived from An Khe by chopper and began to serve breakfast. I could smell the food cooking and this was a real treat since we did not have hot meals in the field. This morning, we would get more rations for later, mail distribution and some hot cereal or SOS and coffee. This was really living.

After breakfast, I told the platoon sergeant about my observation in the night and we started to look around for any signs of rodents or whatever. Looking over the ground, I noticed several holes in the ground the diameter of my thumb and I began to remember. When at Fort Sill, Oklahoma, one summer camp, we were given an orientation about wildlife and insects found there on the reservation and how to be careful. I told the platoon sergeant those holes looked familiar, almost like spider holes. His eyes perked up and he wanted to know what kind of spider. I said, "Holes this big can only mean big spiders like tarantulas." His eyes got even bigger when I said this. He started backing up; I told him not to be alarmed and that I would dig a small hole around this entry and see if we could find what it was for sure.

As I began to extract some soil around the hole, a number of troops began to congregate around me. I told the Native American squad leader what I was doing and he proceeded to help with the digging. When we got down 12 inches or so, we could see something was there, but not until we went down further did the spider jump up out of his hiding place. He just sat there looking at us and he was the size of a small grapefruit in diameter. The corporal wanted to know what to do with it. We discussed delivering it a hundred yards away, but this would only aggravate the spider and he would be back for sure. After some discussion, we executed it by spraying the spider with insect repellent and throwing a match at him.

After that, the entire platoon began the search for more holes and it turned out, there were many. For hours, all we did was look for holes and dig out these insects until there were no more holes in the vicinity. Everyone slept better the next night, knowing this enemy was eliminated.

This story was never published, but those who were there in 1965 can testify to the truth of both stories. Who knew spiders could also be an enemy during a war!

THE HAWAII STORY

It was a beautiful day in the town of Wahiawa and Bruce Burns decided to go fishing up to the North Shore. He was stationed at Scofield Barracks, the army installation, just north of Honolulu on the island of O'ahu.

Bruce told his wife Carol to take their boys swimming and that he would be home for dinner. If he was lucky, he would have a few fish for the barbeque. He kissed her goodbye and headed out. He loved the North Shore and the beautiful scenery and surroundings. Fishing near the town of Haleiwa had always been good and he was looking forward to a relaxing time catching some fish. His spot was close to a deep dark blue pool just off the beach where he had caught fish before, which were the eating kind. He was fishing with a high test line just in case he tied into something big, otherwise, he would be catching smaller fish.

He arrived after driving through the pineapple groves and parked in the designated area. This was in the late 1960s when the parking was still limited along Highway 83. He had some good bait with him that he had bought at the bait shop down the road. Frozen calamari worked the best; however, after several hours, he had no nibbles left and he did not see any fish swimming around. Strange that he saw no fish, but this happened on occasion. Bruce waded out into the surf another couple of feet to get a better look at what might be going on around the area but he saw nothing.

The sun was out and it was a beautiful balmy day. As he looked up the beach, he saw a man and his dog coming in his direction. They were having a good time throwing the ball and if it went into the surf, the poodle would jump into the surf and retrieve it. Bruce kept an eye on them as they approached so that his fishing line would not get tangled up with the dog as they came bye. They were about thirty yards away when the young man threw the ball into the surf about 20 feet from Bruce. The poodle ran and jumped into the surf and swam about 10 feet to get the ball.

Suddenly, Bruce noticed out of the corner of his eye something bursting out of the water, like what whales do when they are having fun. This monster was not a whale but a giant tiger shark with his jaws open; he reached out and completely swallowed the poodle without any struggle. The jaws closed and the shark was gone back into the surf. It was shocking to see all this happening in a fraction of a second. When Bruce looked at the young fellow on the beach, he was on his knees and crying out to the world, "How could this happen?"

Bruce was in shock since this could very easily have been him in the shark's mouth. When he began to back out of the surf on to the beach, he almost couldn't do it because his legs felt like concrete. He finally fell backwards onto the sandy beach and again could hardly get up. While the adrenaline was at work, his legs seemed to have given up. He looked up and crawled over to where the young man was kneeling. Still on his knees, Bruce asked him if he was okay. The man said he was ruined and penniless now that the dog was gone. This guy has some strong feelings for this dog, but what did he mean by all this gibberish? He was penniless? Bruce sat there next to him and when he was calmer, he asked him what he was talking about. They guy was regaining his composure and said he would explain but he needed a drink. They both got up from the beach and Bruce invited him to his car and got two bottles of coke out of the cooler.

Bruce introduced himself while the man said his name was Roger Wilson and that he was on vacation with his wife Maryanne from California. His wife was back at the hotel, and he needed to get back to her and explain what happened. Bruce interrupted and said he was sure he should report this to the Honolulu police when he got back to the hotel. Bruce asked again what it was about the dog that made him so very upset but Roger said he would tell him later. Bruce then gave Roger his telephone number and told him to call if he needed anything. Roger got out of the car and took off down the beach to where his rental car was parked.

Bruce packed up after all the commotion and decided that this was enough excitement for the day. On his way back to Scofield, he wondered what could have been behind all the outlandish crying and yelling about how Roger was ruined and penniless now that the dog was gone. What could have been the reason for his outburst and screaming? Bruce thought he would discuss this with his wife and see if she would come up with some ideas.

When he arrived, Carol was getting dinner ready for the boys, who were exhausted from their swimming and were hungry as bears. Mark asked where all the fish were while his brother Scott wanted to know how many he caught. He told them he got skunked.

"Skunked, what does that mean?" asked Mark.

"Well, it means I didn't catch anything."

"Okay Dad, I am sorry you didn't catch anything, but next time I want to go with you and help you fish."

"Okay son, I will take you next time."

Then Bruce turned to Carol and said, "I am going up stairs to shower and I want to talk with you after we get the boys ready for bed. Okay?" She nodded her head and knew there was something important he wanted to talk to her about. She detected it in his voice.

After his shower, they got the boys showered, and in their pajamas. Finally, when they had been put to bed, Bruce was ready to talk. He poured them a glass of wine, and he told her the whole story. He asked her what she thought this whole thing was about. "Honey, there is definitely some mystery in this story," Carol responded, "I do not know exactly what it could be, but you have a very intriguing story to tell your friends in intelligence at the headquarters on Monday." The United States Army Hawaii Headquarters is located there in Scofield Barracks and is responsible for the security of the Army and its civilians for O'ahu.

It was a long weekend, or at least it seemed like that for Bruce. On Monday, he went into intelligence and explained what happened. They listened politely and then asked him to keep them in the loop if anything further were to develop and he assured them he would. At noon, he went home for lunch and recounted what had gone on at HQ. Carol surmised that was all they would do since there was nothing more to know. Just about the time Bruce was to return to work, his phone rang.

"Hello." It was Roger on the phone wanting to come over to tell Bruce all about what happened and what help they needed. Bruce winked at Carol and said, "Roger, hold on, I want to ask my wife something."

"Honey, do you think we can invite Roger and his wife for a barbeque tonight?" She nodded her head.

"Roger, I have a great idea, why don't you two come over at 6 p.m. and we will have barbeque. Can you do that?"

"Okay then we will see you at 6."

"Carol, I will come home early this afternoon and help you get ready. Is there anything you need me to pick up at the commissary?"

"No Sweetheart, I have enough of everything except you must figure out what you are serving them for drinks."

"Okay, see you at 4:30. Bye."

Roger and his wife showed up right on time and we all retired to the patio. In Hawaii, the best time of the day is the evening time when it is cool and the stars are out. Roger looked a little nervous as he introduced his wife Maryanne. "Bruce, I want to apologize for keeping you in the dark this long, but I needed to talk with my financial adviser before I said anything. You understand?"

"Yes I do Roger."

"Well I want to tell you why I acted like I did when Fluffy was eaten by the shark. I just lost the fortune of a lifetime. I was in the jewelry business and I had decided to pool all our resources into gems and tour the world for a while before we were going to settle down and start a family."

"Okay, go on."

"So we had our leather repair friend make a collar for Fluffy that opened with a zipper in the collar where we had put diamonds worth one million dollars, all top quality. The collar was full of diamonds and if anyone was trying to steal from us, they could rip open our suitcases and find nothing. There are jewel thieves out there watching and we know it. So we are without any money at present; when we get back to the mainland, we can start over and in a short time, we will have the money. Is it possible you both could loan us $2,000 dollars for our tickets home and in six months, we can pay you back?"

Bruce, looked at Carol and said to Roger, "Let us think about it. For now, let me fix you a drink and we can get dinner started." Bruce and Roger talked while Carol and Maryanne talked and they enjoyed each other's company. After spending some time in the meal prep, Carol said she was willing to trust them, so she told Bruce to go ahead and loan them the money. Bruce agreed and so when the desert ice cream was served, he raised his hand and said, "Roger and Maryanne, Carol and I are in agreement to loan you the money and you can repay us when you can."

"Oh, thank you so much," Maryanne said.

Roger was more emotional and gave Bruce a big hug and a thank you. It was a good time and they parted with, knowing they may never see each other again.

Carol was in bed as Bruce was getting ready and she sat up and said, "Bruce, do you know these people are diamond brokers and are very wealthy with land and property? Maryanne told me they have no bank accounts or anything that can be traced, so most of what they have is in diamonds and gems like rubies and emeralds. They will return our money and with interest, she said. I thanked her for being honest with me and she said she liked us and hoped we could stay in touch with them when we returned to the mainland."

"Thank you love for that information. I think I will not say a thing to intelligence tomorrow."

"That is a good idea sweetheart, because those diamonds they lost could be stolen merchandise."

"Ohh," said Bruce.

A year or so later, Bruce and Carol were working on their lawn when the postman came by. Carol went to the mail box and the postman said he had a few letters and gave them to her. There was a letter from Roger and Maryanne in Chicago, Illinois. She walked over to where Bruce was resting and told him she was opening a letter from Roger and Maryanne. There was a check inside and a note that said, "We are so happy to have met you and to have made friends and having you understand our predicament and our dire need for funds to return home. We thank you very much and for not reporting this to the police. We hope this money with interest will help you. Love, Roger and Maryanne."

P.S. The check was for $10k.

THE PENINSULA HOTEL

Hong Kong

Let's begin this story by setting the stage for those unfamiliar with the military and how the troops anticipate their rest break from combat and how they conduct themselves. It is called R&R, rest and recuperation. In combat mode, every day is about the same; most days are boring just waiting around and then there are interludes of absolute chaos, fear and confusion when engaged in combat. This day-to-day existence is extremely difficult since there is time to think about home and all the missed events. Girlfriends and wives are a constant in the thoughts of their men and live with much anxiety, not knowing for sure they will return home after their thirteen-month tour of duty.

Understand that in-country, there are many troops supporting the combat effort. There are at least 10 support troops to one combatant and neither is excited about them being away from home. So, the R&R break is very appealing and important to them all. Getting away from all the elements of battle, sleeping on the hard ground, bad orders, salt-encrusted fatigues, inclement weather, and not very appetizing C rations coming out of a can packaged years ago. All of these are good reasons for R&R and hopefully a boost to the morale of each soldier.

Before going on R&R, each person was given time to shower and change into clean fatigues. A helicopter ride got us into Tan Son Nha't Int'l and Air Force base, where the men assembled for their flight to China.

Uncertain and excited was the mood of the troops, landing at Hong Kong International Airport this February in 1966. They seemed anxious landing on this very narrow runway with ocean surf on both sides. You couldn't see the runway when approaching, only water and there was serious apprehension. Not a word was said as they disembarked the plane and loaded the bus. You could sense the reserved excitement in the mood of these forty-some soldiers as they watched every turn the bus made on its way to the Peninsula hotel.

Mr. Chung stood in the door-well of the bus, trying to get the attention of the group as the bus jerked along. Raising his voice, he welcomed the men to Hong Kong and told them he was the tailor at the Peninsula Hotel and that if they needed anything, he could help them, especially if anyone needed uniforms. He said he was the best military tailor in the city and to prove it, they needed to stop by his shop in the foyer and check him out. He invited the group for a special Chinese dinner three days hence and told everyone to meet at the tailor shop by six p.m. Just as the bus made the last turn into the hotel entrance, he finished his spiel and wished everyone a pleasant R&R.

Latent excitement was beginning to peak. The men had been in the jungle for at least six months and were mesmerized by the affluent scene. They hadn't seen any women other than a Vietnamese, eaten anything other than combat rations, or experienced anything pleasurable like a hot shower or bed with sheets. Just to be in this big city with all the bustle of civilians moving along the street and some good-looking ones crowding around in the lobby of the hotel was enough to kick up the testosterone in these men. Most of these guys were starved for activity, having been captives in the jungle for so long. They were anticipating the finer amenities such as indoor sanitation, clean sheets, hot showers, clear and purified water, tasty chow and cold drinks, including fresh sweet milk. This quick peek at humanity along the streets from the airport was enough to bring memories of what it was like to be back in the civilized world.

Mr. Chung asked the guys to call him Charlie and shook everyone's hand as they bounced off the bus. No one was paying attention much to what he was saying as they eyed the surroundings of this magnificent hotel lobby. It was opulent with decor and looked similar to the set from the movie, "The King and I." Most of the guys appeared crazed as they proceeded through the lobby. Each one was trying to find his way to the reception desk to get checked in, but was not being too careful about how he got there with all the obstacles, especially the lovely females beautifully dressed and their magnificent fragrances wafting in air at nose level. This abrupt entry into the physically provocative milieu of this stunning environment was really a shock for the senses of these weary warriors.

The biggest distraction was the snack bar, which was in the vicinity of the hotel desk and many of the group bolted in its direction when they saw patrons sitting at tables with all kinds of sandwiches and chips in front of them. The most exciting sight was the tall glasses of milk and milk shakes the customers were drinking. Not to understate the importance of this situation, it was this vision of food and milk that stopped many in their tracks. For instance, the milk was packaged in old-fashioned quart glass bottles and many, without even asking for service, helped themselves to a whole quart from the cooler, downing it in several gulps. Cold dairy fresh milk was something that they hadn't enjoyed in over six months.

One of the guys said, "This is the best milk I've ever tasted and I'm a dairy farmer from Wisconsin." The guys dug in and ordered what they wanted but the wait for the food was excruciating.

Finally, after marauding the snack bar and leaving it in shambles, those who couldn't control their appetites began to head again in the direction of the hotel desk. The youngest colonel, who was in charge of the group was leading everyone in that direction. "Guys," he said, "Whatever you do, don't get into any trouble and have a great time. I will meet you back here at this desk six days from now at 6 a.m. Are there any questions?"

Most of the men gave the colonel a half way salute and headed out in different directions. One of the majors looked over at a lieutenant and said he was going to take a crap on a princely throne, light up his cigar and start the evening with Chivas Regal on the rocks all at the same time. When that was over, he would decide what to do next. There were several officers standing close by who overheard his comment and acknowledged it as a good place to start. "Aye Sir," they said.

Three of the young lieutenants agreed to put on the civvies they had brought with them and head uptown to see the sights. After checking in, they met in the tailor shop to get briefed on any good places to see and where to eat reasonably. Mr. Chung was in perfect form meeting and greeting everyone and making them feel like family, offering them a beer or cocktail before they got on their way. He told them that it was a wide-open city and a fun place to shop and sight-see. He suggested they not take all their money with them in case they were to lose it somehow. He suggested they put some of it in the hotel safe. This was an excellent suggestion and many of the guys did just that. When the beers were gone, the three lieutenants headed up the street toward the center of town.

Mike Murphy, the senior first lieutenant who was a few years older than the other two lieutenants, was leading the three and really excited to be away from the jungle and its stench and able to enjoy the fresh air of the sea coast, as the city of Hong Kong is spread out on the coast of the Pacific Ocean. It was late afternoon and they decided to go up town to sight-see and find a good restaurant. They walked a mile looking at every storefront, not necessarily to buy anything, but just to look at everything like children do when accompanying their parents on a shopping spree. The three were having a great time and decided to stop and have a beer.

There were many bars along the street mixed in with the retail stores. Some of these prestigious establishments had good-looking doormen on the sidewalk working hard to solicit pedestrians to enter their establishment. Free entertainment, they advertised, and the cheapest whiskey in town. Not too far down the street, there were several of these escorts standing at the doors of each establishment, in miniskirts with bosoms overflowing their costumes, motioning for the guys to try out the ambiance and they went in.

It was jumping with a three-man band of sorts and many young women in short miniskirts and high, high heels. They were all over the guys with where they should sit and who would sit next to whom. After they got settled, it was time to select drinks. This was not easy for them due to their inexperience in an oriental bar, but after ordering drinks for themselves and for another six ladies who were going to sit with them, they settled down for introductions. Judy, Jean, Beebe, Connie, Chu Chi and Bobbie were all in their late twenties from what could be determined in the limited light of the bar. They were friendly all right and they loved to dance as they gently searched every inch of their dancing partner's body and caressed it more than once. It was socially the right thing to do and following the girls' lead, the guys' hands caressed every voluptuous curve they could find.

The second round of drinks was even more expensive than the last, but they were having fun. The whole shindig was turning out to be very expensive, but what the heck, they thought. The conversation was now getting more serious about what the guys were doing later. Did they have a place to sleep and were they planning to party all night? As the music died down at one point and drinks were being talked about for the third time, the guys whispered they would be broke if they went another round and then they would not have enough money for dinner. They stood up, smiled and thanked the girls for a great time and started for the door. The girls resisted and grabbed the guys, holding on to them and crying for them to stay.

Then, a couple of Chinese men came out from behind the bar to help persuade them to stay and play with the girls. The girls would be very good to them from now on since they knew what they wanted. With some girls still hanging on, they made it to the door and finally out onto the sidewalk. It was a miracle they made it out as they looked at each other in amazement. "We almost didn't get out of there in one piece," exclaimed Pete. "We had better be more careful where we go next or we will be broke in a couple of days," said Mike as they headed down the street looking for a good Chinese restaurant.

They walked past several restaurants and then stepped into the China Grill. It looked clean and there were no hostesses from what they could tell.

The waiter sat them down and they ate some of everything on the menu. It was the best chow they had in the last six months and they washed it down with several bottles of some kind of oriental beer. When they were finished, they looked at each other and decided to head back to the hotel. Mike and Pete checked their pockets for remaining cash while Jim said up that he had hidden a twenty-dollar bill in his shoe for just this situation. "Let's get a taxi and get the hell out of here," he said.

When they arrived at the Peninsula Hotel, what looked like a party was starting with many beautiful ladies meandering in the lobby, mostly with drinks in their hands. The hotel bellhop told them if they wanted to hear some good music, they needed to take the elevator to the top floor, the Eagle's Nest restaurant and nightclub. He said it was a great place to drink and watch the ladies.

Up to the top floor, they went after drawing out more money from the hotel safe. The view of the entire city, the bay and the airport was spectacular. It was so fantastic that they got a table near the window where they could see all the lights and the ocean ferries carrying people across the bay. They ordered drinks and lo and behold, they spotted several tables with just women eating and drinking together. They seemed to be enjoying themselves and the music was especially mellow.

"The bellhop was right," Pete said and the others agreed. This was a great night-club and from the looks of the clientele, the possibilities were limitless. The waitress was very pretty and looked Eurasian with gorgeous brown hair and brown eyes the size of silver dollars. She was perfect in every way and spoke the softest, pure English they had ever heard. When she asked for their order, they asked her for her recommendation since they had already eaten. She said that the best drink they were serving was a Starboard Light made with gin and cream DeMint. It was very tasty and if they didn't like it, she would bring them something else. They decided to take her suggestion and as they were sitting there, they noticed many eyes glancing in their direction. Remember, these guys were well-tanned and very athletic-looking in their lean physiques. Just as these ladies stood out, so did these three great-looking yanks, as they were later to be called.

An hour passed and they had another round of drinks. These were real cocktails with genuine alcohol and perfectly prepared. After the one drink, they began to feel a bit jolly and were having fun making eye contact with the ladies at the surrounding tables. Several were more their mother's age, but looked well cared for and certainly worth smiling at. Who knows if they might have a daughter their age that they might let date a man on R&R. However, there were several tables with two or more women in their late thirties or early forties with amazing bodies easily detected through the sheer fabric partially covering their exquisite physiques. When they stood up to visit the ladies' room and passed by their table, there were only a few details left for the imagination. They had long, shapely legs and firm, round, voluptuous breasts. This wasn't a fashion show, but the ladies were putting on a good one for the guys and they knew the men were enjoying every minute of it. There were several other men at the bar soaking up all this feminine pulchritude and enjoying it as well.

Another hour passed before the band arrived and the crowd began to shift around as the lights began to dim. It was the night club scene coming into bloom and the music began. To illustrate what happened next, the Indians who had been quietly minding their own business before at the bar were on the search for eligible dance partners. The men at the bar were quickly surveying the eligible ladies, heading to their tables and asking for a dance. None of the ladies were so forward enough to ask any of the guys to dance, but there was a subtle invitation with every smile and eye contact. The message was clear about what the ladies wanted. Who was going to be the first to ask any one of them to dance was the question.

Pete decided he could do this, got up and as he headed for his target, he looked back at the guys and blurted out, "Every man for himself." He was a very handsome guy with shoulders like a lumber jack and a twenty-eight-inch waist. He was a pole-vaulter in high school and proud of his physique. As he continued in the direction of his target, there was a slight hush in the audience. He stopped at a table where there were three gorgeous women in their mid-thirties. He asked the blond to dance and both she and the brunette stood up. He was such a gentleman, and with a big smile, he looked the brunette straight in the eyes, "I will be back and you are next my love." He let it slip, his demure was exposed. He had not planned on saying the word, 'love,' but feeling a little light-headed after three Starboard lights, it came out. He hoped it hadn't offended the lady and that she would still be ready for the next dance. As he was dancing with the blond, he noticed another man stop at the table and then walk away.

His dance partner, Ruth, was named by her father; she was from Indiana and working at the American consulate. She was single and a great dancer. Her friends were single as well. Where was Pete from and why was he here in Hong Kong? She asked him. Pete almost missed the question, thinking and feeling this slender body magnetically enticing his own and with the perfume of champions in his nostrils, his blood sizzled. The effect was similar to a shot of morphine and the delirious impact it had on his body—total intoxication. He heard the question, but did not comprehend it. He asked her to repeat the question if she would and she did with a smile. He said he wasn't concentrating and she understood. He said, he was from California and his parents lived in San Diego. He was in the U.S. Army and on R&R. What more did she want to know? She pressed herself closer as they danced slowly and told him she did not know any soldiers, but was impressed with this one.

"Are all soldiers trained to dance so well?" she asked. He squeezed her gently and brushed her ear with his lips as he answered, "No." He could feel excitement and trembling in her loins. He stopped talking when the music stopped and took her hand as he led her to the table. He pulled out her chair and held it as she sat down, then he leaned over and gave her a very gentle kiss on the cheek and thanked her for the dance. He smiled at her friend and said he would be back for the next dance. The band took a ten-minute break.

As the guys arrived back at their table, they agreed to order another round of drinks. Pete was asked, "How did it go with the blond?" Mike and Jim had danced with beautiful ladies, but they were a little older than them; some six to eight years older but very well-preserved. They had to have been beauty queens in college and except for their age, they looked positively beautiful. Pete is the one who had danced with the blond who looked the same age as him. Yes, she was close to his age and from Indiana, working there in Hong Kong for the American Consulate. All the gals were single and Pete planned to dance next with the brunette. By the way, had he said that his first dance was with Ruth and one of them should dance with her next? She was a sensuous dancer and if the brunette was anything like Ruth, they may have discovered gold in human form.

The band was back and they started with a Glenn Miller song, slow and gentle. Pete motioned for Mike to follow him to the table, which he did and as Pete leaned over to ask the brunette to dance, Mike asked Ruth. They both smiled and stood up, giving their hand to the guys. As they walked to the dance floor, the brunette lightly squeezed Pete's hand and placed it on her buttock as they reached the dance floor. He pulled her close as they began to dance and her perfume sent an electric shock through his body.

Whatever brand of perfume it was, it must have had a name such as Toxic or Poison or maybe Prisoner. It was toxic, acting like poison and he was definitely a prisoner ready for torture. He mused, *oh! What torture could she inflict?* And, as they danced, he found out her name was Marion and she was a good friend of Ruth's. They had been friends from high school and went to college together. They continued dancing for another few minutes and then the band stopped.

As he returned her to her table, he asked if he and his buddies could join them for a nightcap. Marion looked at Ruth and they both looked to their friend Beth, who nodded in the affirmative. As Pete and Mike returned to their table to retrieve their drinks and invite Jim to accompany them, they noticed him at another table talking with two ladies sitting at one end of the restaurant lounge. They waved at him and returned to the ladies' table. They sat together on one side, and the three gals sat on the other.

The conversation continued for a period of time about the best places to see and where the best shopping was on the Kowloon side of the bay. The ladies were very nice and interested in showing them around if they wanted. Ruth spoke up that she would like to go too, but she had to work the next day. The guys agreed to meet Beth and Marion for a shopping spree in Kowloon in the morning and then all the negotiations began as to where to meet. Ruth said she would get the girls to the Grand Hotel by 9 a.m. and that the guys should meet them there.

It was close to midnight and the ladies needed to get going if they were to catch the last ferry home. Ruth picked up the conversation and told the guys how much she enjoyed meeting them and if they were going to be around for a few days, she might get to see them again. She hoped the four of them would have a super time shopping and she wished she could go along. The guys walked the gals down to the lobby and out to the front door. The bell captain ushered them to a waiting taxi and the gals, all three, gave

Pete and Mike kisses on the cheek and big hugs. They got in the cab and waved as they departed. Pete waved back as they went out of sight. Now back to the Eagle Nest to find their buddy, Jim.

Jim was just where they last saw him talking with two women and they meandered over to say hello. As they approached, Jim stood up and greeted them and introduced them to the ladies. One was considerably older than the other and what they found out was Mildred was Veronica's mother and they were visiting from Australia. Her son was in the Australian army and assigned to the Australian consulate in security. Veronica and her mother were there on vacation to see her son. Mildred was a good looker for being in her fifties and Veronica was in her mid-twenties and a real bombshell. She was about five-foot-five and had the bluest eyes and the blackest hair. She was soft-spoken and she asked if they would like to sit down, which they did. Again, drinks were in order and the ladies had beer. Being from Australia, they were big on their beer and so the guys had a beer as well. Time was getting on and after drinking the beer, Pete and Mike said goodnight and told Jim to meet them for breakfast at the snack bar at eight if he could make it.

Pete and Mike were in rooms opposite one another on the fifteenth floor with views of the entire city. They wondered about Jim and decided to get the low down from him in the morning. They said they would call each other in the morning, whoever woke up first. They were actually completely worn out after this first day and were looking forward to a good night's sleep on a full-size mattress, but before bed, a hot shower was in order. They said goodnight to each other and entered their rooms.

The next morning they met as planned and were at the snack bar around eight. Jim did not show up, and they wondered about him. Had he gone home with the ladies, maybe got waylaid on the street, or what? They were worried and decided to find out his room number, which was on another floor. The concierge helped them to find Jim's room number and they called him. He did not answer, so they went ahead and had some breakfast before they left for the Grand Hotel. Real milk in their cereal was like being in heaven and real to-goodness fresh ground coffee that smelled and tasted fantastic. It was like being home again, which brought memories to mind and a slight sadness to them both. They wished they were home, but the thought of another six months in the jungle gave them a tinge of melancholy. They were not really excited about going back, but this was enough serious thinking. They were here to have a great time and entertain themselves and the ladies.

As Pete and Mike headed to the ferry by taxi, they discussed which of the gals they liked. Were they going to pair up or just let things work themselves out? They discussed this for a few minutes and decided they would let nature run its course and see what happened. The ferry ride was fun and it took only about fifteen minutes to get across the bay. It was a four-decker and held maybe a thousand passengers, maybe a little less. Getting aboard and off went well. It didn't take more than five minutes to disembark. It was the crowd on the street that made it difficult to make any time, but with directions given to them the night before, they were going to make it okay.

When they arrived at the hotel, they were feeling a little excited about what exactly was going to take place. Spending the day with these gals shopping wasn't what they had in mind doing on their R&R, but what else did they have going? It was possible they would have a fantastic time, and so they attacked the idea with gusto. When they came in the door, the gals were right there waiting for them with big smiles and looking like a million bucks in their beautiful, attractive sundresses.

"Where did you guys get so tanned this time of year?" asked Mike, and the gals, in unison, said they had been in Mexico for a week before coming to visit Ruth.

"Oh," the guys said in unison, "How great."

They smiled again and each one took a hand of the guys and headed out the door.

"Let us show you the sights today and let's have a good time," Beth said. Marion spoke up and added, "We want you soldiers to have a great time while you're here and we need to help you do that, have a great time." They all smiled at each other and headed off to the best shopping in the world, just a few blocks away.

They went into the alleyways between the big buildings where many a vendor displayed their wares. It wasn't hard finding anything they wanted—from luggage to leather purses and jackets and custom leather dresses, shoes to sunglasses, binoculars, jewelry and furs—anything you could want was at your fingertips. All of them had fun talking with the vendors and after a full morning of shopping, they agreed to lunch at some good restaurant. Where would they take them? The guys wondered. The gals, only a couple of weeks in town, knew where they were going and not far from this alleyway market was a special place Ruth had taken her friends a week ago. It was not a cafe or grill and the ambiance was superb. The guys were impressed when they entered the Imperial Palace Hotel. This is one of the most exquisite buildings in Hong Kong and maybe in the Orient, with dark-skinned doormen six foot tall in their Indian soldier's uniform with gold epaulets and with white fur hats 24 inches tall. They were impressive and the foyer was even that much more elegant. The gals held their hands tight and escorted them to the restaurant looming ahead,

The Royal Empress. It was something to behold, with tables for a thousand and tablecloths with gold accents and gold everywhere. The Mai-tre'd were dressed in tuxs and seated them at a window so they could see the bay and all the ocean traffic. Service was only a step away as each table had a waiter, a water boy, a server and a girl as a busboy. They couldn't sip their water without it being refilled immediately.

They began with light cocktails and feasted on a grand lunch of fresh salmon. The lunch took two hours and it was an experience of a lifetime. The guys were amazed by it all and had a great time entertaining the ladies with every witty story they could remember and a few they made up. They didn't want to go and so spent the better part of the afternoon drinking Empress Tea and beer with many trips to the restroom. The ladies seemed impressed that on the other side of the world, they were being entertained by two magnificent species of Homo Erect-us who were smart and entertaining warriors at their best.

Jim was on the other side of the bay with his two lady friends, Mildred and Veronica. They, too, had been shopping and had finally decided to stop for lunch at a small Chinese chop house or cafe. They had a marvelous time shopping and the ladies really had a good time. Jim suggested that he get back to the hotel so he could purchase some uniforms and they should return to his hotel for drinks and dinner later that evening. Veronica looked at her mother for approval and got it. It was settled, the two of them were meeting Jim for dinner, and they were going to meet in his room for cocktails before they decided which restaurant they would go to. Jim hugged the two women and told them to have a good afternoon and he was looking forward to meeting them around seven p.m. He noticed that Veronica was very alert to his hug and placed her bosom against his chest as they embraced. She was warm and placed a slender kiss on his cheek as they separated.

They said goodbye with some reluctance and told Jim they would look forward to the evening's activities. Jim's plan was to find the Major and get him to come with them as Mildred's escort, and he needed to get back to the hotel to make that happen.

Jim headed back and when he arrived, he decided to check in with Charlie at the tailor shop. There was a crowd there getting measured and having their feet measured for new shoes. It was a full-service operation and very well organized. They immediately recognized him and called him by name and fetched him a cold Heineken. Then Charlie asked him what he had in mind and Jim wanted a khaki dress blouse and pants. There were several field grade officers who had this uniform and it was really sharp. Charlie had one of his assistants start measuring Jim and in fifteen minutes, he was done. On second thought, Jim ordered two additional khaki shirts that he could wear in summer. All told, his estimate for the uniforms was a little over a hundred dollars. Wow, that was unbelievable. He smiled at Charlie and Charlie told him to come in the next afternoon for his fitting.

The tailors worked around the clock in the building across the street. Jim was amazed and while he was there, the Major came in. Jim immediately went over to him and began the conversation. The major had been out shopping for his wife and had bought some gold jewelry, a bracelet and a neck chain in 18kt gold and they were beautiful. Jim asked him if he was busy that evening and the major asked him why. Jim told him the story and said he couldn't just ask the daughter without the mother. After some deliberation, the major said, "What the heck, I'll make it a foursome."

Jim thanked him and told him to come to his room at seven for cocktails. The major gave him a thumbs up and headed to the snack bar. Jim headed for his room after speaking with the concierge. He needed a half bottle of gin and a half bottle of Jim Beam to start. He thought he would make them all an Old-fashioned, which was a fairly common drink in those days. The concierge suggested that he order a cocktail cart with everything he might need and they would bill him for only what he used. "Great idea," Jim said, and headed to his room. The booze cart was arranged for delivery around six thirty.

Up in the room, he began to feel the effects of all the fun he had been experiencing and decided to lay down for a short nap. Before he did, he called the desk and asked to be called at six p.m. and he dropped on the bed like a ton of potatoes. He didn't wink for two hours and hardly knew why the phone was ringing. The operator said it was time to call and that while he was sleeping, he received a message. It was from Pete and Mike telling him they were planning for him to accompany them for dinner and be Ruth's escort. He rang Pete's room and left him a message that he was already booked for the evening and couldn't make it. He was having dinner with the ladies from Australia and the Major. Sorry, he couldn't make it. They were, however, invited to come to his room for cocktails at seven and to call him when they arrived back at the hotel.

That evening turned out great, with everyone arriving on time and cocktails being made by one of the staff attendants. This was a nice treat and it cost ten dollars to have the bartender make the drinks. The conversation was lively and after an hour, the four went to dinner at the best Indian restaurant in town, the Taj Mahal.

Upon arrival, we were escorted to a table nearest the window looking out over the bay. It was a magnificent view of the entire waterfront and all the ships and boats moving along with lights, millions of lights showering the entire waterfront. The ladies were very impressed and the discussion turned to the menu and what to select. As the waiter arrived in all his exquisite attire and white tux dinner jacket, he bowed and welcomed them to his table, where they would be his guests to serve. He sounded like an American without any accent and he asked us for our drink order. They were impressed!

They ordered and dined until they were all stuffed. Everything was delicious and after dinner, they had cordials. Now it was close to 10 p.m. and the major suggested they all go back to the Eagle's Nest bar on the top floor of their hotel. All of them agreed they had time for a nightcap before the ladies needed to be at the ferry to get back to their hotel, where they were staying somewhere on the other side of the bay. Everything went as planned and after the nightcap, they caught a cab back to the ferry. Before they left, a plan was hatched that they would get together the following afternoon for cocktails at the Royal Hong Cong Hotel.

Before Veronica got into the taxi, she needed a private moment with Jim and as she leaned against him, she whispered in his ear, "You are very handsome and loving and I want to know you better." Jim suggested she call him in the morning and they would hatch a plan to do that. He again lightly caressed her back and buttocks as he kissed her on the neck and opened the door to the taxi.

The next morning came early. The body felt tender and the brain was foggy acting. But, after coffee and sweet rolls at the snack bar, Jim was ready for his fitting at the tailor shop. Mr. Chung greeted him at the door and ushered him to a room off to the side for his fitting. As Charlie watched the proceedings, he asked about how everything was going and how Jim liked Hong Kong. He told him it was an exciting place, and he needed to buy something for his wife. He took Jim next door to a ladies' boutique, where he explained my wife's size, weight and height. They immediately began making a silk suit in green. The fabric was unbelievable, shiny green silk. It turned out to be one of the real buys there in Hong Kong. Fifty bucks and it was ready the next day. This tailoring work was processed 24/7 around the clock and the finished work was exquisite.

This was a good test of masculine fortitude, giving in to all the pleasures of this R&R, preparing oneself for another six months in-country fighting the elements and the NVA. It was stressful, but they did the right thing and got the men notified to be ready to depart the next day.

The morning was rushing on and Veronica needed a telephone call. Back in the room, she was called and she softly answered like a whispering angel waiting expectantly for her lover to call. She was very excited to hear Jim's voice and she wanted to visit him right away. He agreed and waited anxiously for her to knock on his door. It was a one-of-a-kind meeting and at the door, she engaged him in a kiss of passion and pushed him back into the room.

Several hours later, she called her mom and told her she would be home later and to go ahead and have dinner without her. What she didn't tell her mother was she had been feasting all afternoon on human flesh.

Roll call came early that next morning on the bus. They were really leaving and no one was missing. Oh God! What a wonderful experience, they all thought as there was excited talk about all the adventurous escapades the guys experienced.

Veronica had exchanged her address with Jim and their relationship endured for several months of correspondence until the truth came out. End of story.

THE UNEXPECTED DRIVE

This story takes place in 2001 when Bob and June Wheeler decide to visit their longtime friends in San Ramon, California. The Wheelers were neighbors with the Craigs in Castro Valley, California, when Bob Wheeler got out of the army. They became the best of friends thirty-five- plus years ago and their children attended the same neighborhood school. The Wheelers had visited two or three times in the past, but it had been eight years since they had been together. They wanted to see the Craig's children, Karen and Larry and see how they matured.

Bob and June were off to the Denver International Airport. They anticipated a fantastic week of reunion with lunches at the wharf in San

Francisco. The best of the best in seafood is found in the small settlement along the wharf in San Fran. After picking up the Wheelers, the Craigs headed for their favorite spot, the Lighthouse restaurant, which rested on the rocky crest overlooking the Pacific Ocean.

It was great to see the Craigs again. There were more than enough hugs and kisses to go around. They enjoyed their dinner and the conversation never stopped. Dinner was excellent, as always. This was a good time for the families to catch up on each other and much of the discussion needed pictures that were at home in San Ramon. After dessert, the group headed back to San Ramon, where the Craigs lived in their new ranch home. The reminiscing was lively in the car, but Bob noticed that June was getting quiet and that was not her way. She had been so excited that they were making this trip to visit their long-time best friends. June was becoming agitated and wanted to rest, she told Bob. He kept his eye on her, wondering if she was alright. In a few minutes, he asked her if she was okay and she wanted to rest her head in his lap. She said, "I am feeling very peculiar and thought I might lay my head in your lap since I feel so tired." She did look exhausted and weak. She put her head on Bob's lap and he sensed something was really wrong. It wasn't like June to become this tired so quickly, he thought as he watched her intently. Her breathing became shallow and she was very placid. June was not communicating. She was having trouble understanding his simple questions and was not able to dialog with him. Bob said, "Bruce, June is not well and I need you to drive us to the closest ER." Bruce perked up, "We are close to the San Ramon Medical Center and I will be there in minutes." In the ten minutes it took to arrive there, June fell into unconsciousness and was barely breathing.

The doctor on duty at San Ramon Medical Center took charge and immediately began life support measures to keep June breathing. At this time, Bob heard the doctor call for numerous lab tests to determine the cause of her condition. They drew blood samples every few minutes to test for toxins, allergies and poisons, all with negative results. The doctor showed concern and stepped into the hall outside the ER, where Bob and the Craigs anxiously waited. It wasn't a good prognosis. The test proved that what they were trying to find as the cause was elusive. The doctor said, "There could be some type of foreign virus causing June's problem, but my team hasn't figured it out yet," and June continued on a downward spiral.

At about 10:00 a.m. the next morning, June was removed from life support equipment. Dr. Griffin said, "This is the most extraordinary medical emergency that I and the staff have ever experienced". She actually broke down in the waiting room when she told them that the virus attacked the lungs with paralysis and that they wanted to begin an autopsy to determine the cause, which Bob adamantly refused. He was devastated by this tragedy. His loss was overwhelming. He needed to rest before he could think of what to do next. He was mumbling to himself, "Oh my God," as he left the room.

Bob was broken-hearted and depressed. He looked devastated, like his life was coming to an end. His complexion was acrid white, showing his purple veins bulging out of his temples. He believed God had vanished and was no longer by his side to comfort him. He felt God abandoned him and he was confused. How could God allow this to happen? Many of Wheeler's friends in the Bay were at the hospital to help because Bruce had called them. They were devastated as well and, at this time, were of little help in comforting Bob. He was just one step from total despair and it showed in his countenance. His mind was spinning out of control and emotionally, he was drained. How could he live without June, his love of forty-five years?

Bruce asked, "Bob, what is there for me to do? What can I help you with my friend? I want to help and I think we should ask God to give you direction and solace. This kind of tragedy comes along seldom in a person's life and I want to help you see that. God is not angry with you or has forsaken you. So, what do you need? Just say it and Joyce and I will try to find the way for you. Would you like us to fly home with you?" But, Bob just stood there with a ghostly stare on his face, without saying anything.

June was received the following day at the Heavenly Hills Mortuary, where she was prepared for burial. The mortician was most sympathetic and wanted to be of help. He advised Bob concerning the details in preparation for June's flight to Denver on the 11th. The airlines made the reservation for 4:00 p.m. that day. Bob was apprehensive about the flight for some reason. His nerves were shattered. Around 9:00 a.m. that morning, while packing, his friend Bruce called him to drop everything and come see what was on TV. The Twin Tower event was splashed all over the screen and on every network.

This is where Bob Wheeler was riveted in shock as the events of that morning proceeded in horror.

His original flight had been canceled; now, a day later, on Wednesday the 12th of September, Bob was slow to get started. He called the airlines, "Sir, we are not sure about anything due to this tragedy." They couldn't tell him anything definite. They weren't able to tell him even if they were going to fly that day. So his request to book a flight the following day went nowhere, and the phone went dead.

Bob asked Bruce, "What should I do?" Bruce called the mortuary and talked with the manager, "What are Bob's options?" The manager said, "I can arrange transport for June, by hearse with licenses for interstate travel to Colorado if you want?"

After conferring with his friend, Bob decided it was now or never. He called the manager back and accepted the proposed plan. The manager would get one of his qualified drivers to transport the body to Denver. Bob would go along and help the driver with directions since he was very familiar with the road to Denver. The following day, on the 13th, Bob and the hearse began their journey back to Denver after emotional goodbyes with the Craigs.

Tom Thornburg was the driver selected. He was a single young man in his early thirties. He told Bob, "I was trained in the Army as a tank driver in the recent Desert Storm conflict." He assured Bob that after his stint in combat driving vehicles, he was qualified to get them to Denver safely. Bob and Tom made good time that first day and were in Winnemucca, Nevada before nightfall.

As Bob placed his suitcase in the back of the hearse the next morning, he noticed the container in which June's body was placed for transport was disturbed. The shipping container had a lid and it was ajar as if someone was searching for something and left suddenly without closing it completely. June's body was on its side as if someone had moved her. He thought this was strange but he didn't say anything to Tom about it. They had another successful day of driving and arrived in Laramie, Wyoming, where they spent the night at the Sunset Motel.

Bob didn't sleep at all well, remembering his discovery earlier that morning. He wondered if June was trying to convey to him some thought telepathically like she had many times in their married life. What could be the message though? They had been very close in their forty-plus years of marriage and many times, they had the exact same thought, at the same time. So what was June trying to tell him?

As he opened the back of the hearse to store his travel bag, there was the container lid ajar and slightly open. The body was in another position. He noticed her hand was exposed and he saw that her wedding ring was missing. Now what could have happened to her ring? He knew it was on her hand when they put her in the box, but now where was it?

As soon as Tom returned from paying their night's lodging, Bob asked, "Tom, when we first started, do you remember how my wife looked when we first put her in this shipping container?

"What do you mean asked Tom?"

"Well, do you remember what she was wearing and any jewelry she may have been wearing?"

Tom looked a little confused but thought a moment. He looked up at Bob and asked, "What exactly are you asking me Bob?" Tom was thinking maybe Bob suspected him of stealing his wife's ring. Bob was actually looking for some confirmation of his wild idea that the corpse was somehow trying to send him a message. He asked Tom if it would be okay to search the container for the ring. As Bob took a preliminary look in the open area around June, he did not find anything. It was then that he talked with Tom about the position he found the body the night before and how he had just noticed the lid on the box partially ajar and her wedding ring missing from her finger.

Tom answered, "I'm not really sure what I remember, but I thought she was wearing her wedding ring when we placed her in the container. As far as the container being opened and moved, I don't know how that happened." Tom thought maybe the change of position of the body was due to June's weight shifting around as they drove over the road. So he told Bob, "Don't worry yourself Bob. There are no ghosts and you are still in shock over this whole ordeal."

Bob thanked Tom and dropped the subject. As they got into the hearse, Bob smelled the scent of June's favorite perfume. Bob looked startled and Tom asked Bob what was bothering him. Bob shook his head and said he was not bothered about anything. He didn't want to get into another conversation with Tom about these weird things that were happening.

Bob was so moved by this whole episode and by what he saw in the ashtray he could hardly hold on to his emotions. Tom asked again, "Bob do you want me to start us out or should we stop across the street and have another coffee?" Bob nodded his head and looked again into the ashtray. There were candy wrappers in the tray that were not there yesterday. These wrappers were from the type of candy June carried with her when she needed a boost due to her low blood sugar. This was just another jolt that was very difficult for Bob. June was a diabetic for many years and was always eating this type of hard candy to bump up her blood sugar. Bob said nothing to Tom about this; since this was the last leg of their journey, Bob told Tom he would take the wheel since he knew the way from there onwards. As they took off for Denver, Bob could not get his mind off this mystery. It was weird how these clues June was leaving were so real, yet her message was hidden.

They were just north of Fort Collins on Highway I-25 when Bob heard a loud bang and the vehicle sank down in the left rear. They realized they had a flat and pulled over. They both got out and looked under the hearse for the spare tire and to their surprise, there was none. Hearses were usually not going cross country and so, no replacement tire was on board. Bob took a minute and then called AAA, which he had maintained since 1980. It was the best insurance he and June had ever taken out and they had used it several times while traveling the country. When he got the operator, she told him there was a wait and it could be close to two hours due to the shortage of drivers that day. He agreed AAA should come ahead when they could and the sooner, the better. The temperature this day was uncommonly warm for mid-September and with June not in refrigeration, it was imperative to move quickly. Next, Bob called his son, Scott, who had been briefed on the entire episode of his mother's death and told him to get Bob's Cadillac and drive a few miles north of Fort Collins and pick them up along the road. The reason for this was that they were not sure when

AAA would get there. Scott told his dad he would be there as soon as he could, which could be in about an hour.

When Scott arrived in little more than an hour, Bob was delighted to see him. They embraced and wept together for a short time. Bob thanked Scott profusely for his effort and lightning speed. Then he discussed with Scott that their best plan of action would be for Scott to stay with Tom and the hearse and show him the way to their house after the tow to the gas station and tire repair. There would be time then to arrange for Tom's early departure back to San Francisco the next day. Scott agreed and they loaded June into the back seat of the yellow 1990 Cadillac Seville. Bob didn't have time to tell Scott the weird incidents that had taken place, but there would be time later when they arrived home.

After the tire repair by AAA, Scott and Tom were finally on their way. AAA had beaten their time estimate and the hearse was on the way to Denver about 90 minutes later. Not 10 miles down the road, they came upon a horrendous traffic accident with numerous vehicles, maybe four, five or more, all mangled and in a heap. This was just outside of Fort Collins, south of town. Fire trucks and ambulances were everywhere. The highway patrol was directing traffic and Scott noticed what looked like his dad's yellow Cadillac in the pile-up. Scott jumped out of the hearse almost before it stopped and ran over to the nearest patrol officer, who confirmed two persons had been removed from the Cadillac and had been taken to Denver General Hospital. The officer couldn't tell him anything more because he wasn't in charge.

When Scott arrived at Denver General, he worriedly approached the information desk. "Yes, can I help you?" said the clerk. Scott, visibly on edge, had trouble getting out his request. "Have you received an older couple from the wreck in Fort Collins?" The clerk passed the buck to the other desk person and they told Scott that an ambulance had indeed brought in a couple from the accident named—she paused as she looked at the card—Wilson and they were DOA and are now in the basement vault, waiting to be identified."

Scott, the ex-military man, kept his cool and went directly to the basement to make the I.D. of his parents. There was something unusual about their appearance, he thought. He noticed that they didn't look too banged up for all they had been through in the wreck. His mother's body didn't look bad at all. She was in excellent shape and her hair was not messed up. He remembered looking at her closely when he had earlier helped his dad load her out of the container and lay her down in the back seat of the Cadillac. Now studying her lying there, Scott envisioned a slight grin on her face as if she was smiling at him.

This startled Scott and he began thinking again. He remembered his mother saying that she hoped that she and Dad could go together when the time came. She was always saying this to him. He wondered how strange it was that both his parents were now dead and each from a different cause. Still, it was mysterious how they were together there on separate gurneys, facing each other in the same vault. She was smiling at his dad. Could this be a message to him as well that she had accomplished her wish and they both were together again and would remain together throughout eternity? Scott sighed and signed the papers for the release to the mortuary.

The next day the mortuary attendant from McDougal Mortuary picked up the two corpses and delivered them to the embalming room. Both were laid out on the two tables for the mortician to begin his work. The technician on duty, Dan, began with Scott's father. The process was almost completed when he noticed the woman on the other table. She looked different from the corpse he was working on, her husband. She was very clean and tidy in her dress and exhibited what looked like fresh makeup. How suspicious and as Dan was finishing the man, he looked over quickly at the woman and she had a grin on her face. The grin was a mystery and virtually impossible since facial muscles cannot be configured in any expression after death. At death, all muscles, and especially facial muscles, are totally relaxed and impossible to stage. Dan was more than surprised by all of this and kept watching her while completing his job on the husband. What was it that caused him to flinch each time he looked over at her?

Now it was time to begin on the woman and for some unknown reason, he was very apprehensive about getting started. He began in the normal fashion with implements at the ready for the extraction of blood. Dan made his first incision and no blood, just embalming fluid. Wow! "What is this all about?" he yelled out reflexively. *How could this lady have been embalmed already?* For an instant, he thought she was alive. He believed she moved her lips and wanted to speak to him. His excitement turned to fear and fear into panic. He was frozen in place and couldn't even utter a sound. This type of fright keeps you from thinking clearly and your mind cannot keep up with the impulses of attacking stimuli. You become delirious with fear and the fear engages your senses for rational thinking. This cannot be happening. This corpse is not for real. No blood! Then, the fear and the adrenaline that had you over the top begin to subside and wear off. Rationally, you begin to think again and you discover this corpse is already dead from another time. She is truly dead and already embalmed and prepared for burial. *What kind of cynical joke is this?*

Later that morning, the mortician, Dan, noticeably rattled, was taking a break when the manager came into the break room. The manager began relating some of the gory details of the ten-car pile-up the day before. One eye witness told the highway patrol he believed the accident was caused by the lady driving the yellow Cadillac, who crossed the median and hit the oncoming car head-on. Her body was found pinned behind the steering wheel and her husband was in the back seat. Dan was visibly moved by this story and jumped out of his chair.

"How could this be?" He screamed at the manager. "The already dead lady was driving! No way Jose! They got it wrong! Dead people can't drive and she was dead, dead, dead!" He screamed. He simply couldn't take it any longer, grabbed his jacket and went out the door, mumbling to himself. "I'm leaving this place and never coming back."

THE END

About the Author

Bill is a conservative person with a multiple job history. Born in NY into a military family, you will see from his stories many different genre of settings. Received his BA at the UC Boulder and married a Colorado girl. They had two sons before he graduated and received his commission into the Army. A year later he was deployed to Vietnam with the 1st Cav. Division. His writing started late, probably in 2002. Now retired and widowed his mind is open to new ventures. He should be telling more contemporary stories in the future. Associated with Western Colorado Writer's Forum.